Cover Your Head!

Blips lit the heat-detection screens of the No Slack Too as the Soviet engines coughed to life. "Fruits," he said, "take the Phalanx on manual and dust 'em up a little." The loader rotated his seat to the Phalanx console and hosed the hill with 37mm depleted-uranium slugs, setting up a hellish cacophony that spurred the Communist tanks into movement. Suddenly a missile hurled in from the fog. Its detonation shattered across the rear deck of the XM-F4, jolting the men inside.

Tag had no choice. His first instinct was to call for a shot, but he had no idea where the Rangers were in relation to the Soviet tanks.

"Gentlemen," he said to his crew, "stand by to ram . . ."

TANKWAR IV:
FIREBRAND

TANKWAR IV:
FIREBRAND

LARRY STEELBAUGH

BERKLEY BOOKS, NEW YORK

TANKWAR IV: FIREBRAND

A Berkley Book / published by arrangement with
the author

PRINTING HISTORY
Berkley edition / October 1991

ISBN: 0-425-12966-7

A BERKLEY BOOK ® TM 757, 375
Berkley Books are published by The Berkley Publishing Group,
200 Madison Avenue, New York, New York 10016.
The name "Berkley" and the "B" logo are trademarks belonging
to Berkley Publishing Corporation.

PRINTED IN THE UNITED STATES OF AMERICA

10   9   8   7   6   5   4   3   2   1

For Julie,
for her support, good humor, and,
when the money's on the table,
her three-rail bank shot

1

Max Tag felt like hell. His mouth was parched, his eyelids were gummed together, and his shoulder was a contusion of pain—distant pain, held in check by the anesthesia that was just beginning to wear off. When he tried to raise his right hand to rub his eyes, the effort against the sutures, tape, and bandages that bound the wounded arm caused a dull pain to radiate from his wound, and he arched his back in agony, unable even to cry out past the tongue that cleaved to the roof of his mouth. Through all this, he struggled to clear his head, remember where he was, what had happened, but the hurt and the drugs blocked out thoughts, leaving him with sensation alone.

From someplace far away he heard a familiar woman's voice say, "Doctor, here. I think he is coming to." Then Tag felt something cool and wet on his face, wiping away the amber from his eyes, pressing a rough wetness to his lips. A chill rippled the length of his body, and he realized that he could move his left hand. He slapped clumsily at his face.

"Easy, Max," he heard the familiar voice say, closer now. "Lie still. The doctor is here, and you are all right."

Even to breathe was difficult, so he did lie still, pinching the last of the sleep from the corners of his eyes before he tried to open them. He blinked and through a blur saw Giesla leaning over him, holding a basin and a damp cloth that she now squeezed and pressed to his mouth.

"Suck a little from this, Max," she said. "Just enough to wet your throat."

He sucked the wet terry cloth greedily and swallowed hard, the way a man who has nearly drowned gulps air. He began to speak and at once remembered Wheels Latta, his driver who had been killed in the ambush by Soviet T-80B tanks behind the line of nuclear devastation, the same ambush where Tag received his wound, and he went limp on the cot, sorrow eating a hollow in his chest.

A man's voice that he did not recognize said, "Hold his head and let him have a drink."

Tag felt strong, slim fingers slide behind his neck and lift his lips to the cold metal rim of a canteen cup. He tried to sip slowly but nearly gagged when he swallowed. Finally he was able to get some down, then more, then he opened his eyes again.

There was Giesla, sitting beside his cot on an ammunition box, her face etched with concern. Behind her stood a man in camouflage uniform, captain's bars sewn on one point of his collar and a caduceus on the other, and over his breast pocket, embroidered jump wings. Tag looked at each of them without speaking, trying to orient himself. He was surrounded by lantern light and parachute silk, in a cool, dim place that smelled of rock and antiseptic. He could hear other indistinct voices from farther away, echoing, muted. Of course—the old mineworks in the Jura. He remembered now. Christ, he felt worse than when he had first been brought in. He remembered drinking Ross Kettle's bourbon with Colonel Barlow, thinking that the next thing he had to do was complete his report for SACEUR and wait for Kettle's orders. Then he had a hypo, came awake hurting before dawn, and had another hypo when Bones, the medic, came to scrub his shoulder. He was still groggy when the doctor arrived and put the mixture of tranquilizers and anesthetic in his veins.

The doctor knelt beside Giesla and said, "How are you feeling, Max?"

Tag blinked, smacked his lips, and looked at him. "A hell of a lot worse than when I came in," he said.

The doctor was a thick-set man with a round, intelligent face. He smiled merrily at Tag and said, "They say I have a heavy hand at table, but I make up for it with my bedside manner. I'm Dr. Harrison, Max. You can call me Bill." He took Tag's left hand to shake it. "I'm the one who patched you up—and you were a mess, mister."

"Great," said Tag. "Glad to hear it."

"You are going to be fine, Max," Giesla said, "only it was a very near thing for you."

"Yeah," Harrison said, "you had a chunk about the size of a cocklebur and ten times sharper riding right on the wall of your jugular, and enough scrap to load a box of shotgun shells in your deltoid and trapezius muscles. You were bad wing-shot, Max; it'll take a few weeks before you start to unlimber; but I'm not recommending you be taken out of the field. Take your antibiotics, and take your painkillers. You'll need them for the next couple of days. You'll mend faster if you do."

"I will see to it," Giesla said.

"Doc," Tag said, "when can I see Colonel Barlow?"

"I'll tell him you've come around," Harrison said as he stood up. "Let's see how you feel this afternoon, after the rest of the anesthesia wears off and you've had something to eat. Nothing but liquids until lunch.

"Lieutenant Ruther," he said to Giesla, "tie him down, if you have to."

Harrison disappeared through a flap in the parachute canopy that had been his surgical suite, and Tag said to Giesla, "Wheels?"

"He's gone home, Max," she said. "I wrote a letter to his family myself. I told them there would be one from you to follow, and I told them why."

"Good," Tag said. "I'm glad they'll get one from somebody who knew him. Wait—do you mean this morning?"

"Yesterday, Max. You slept around the clock."

"Where's the crew? N. Sain? Prentice?"

"Fine, everyone is fine, Max. And they all want to see you," Giesla said. "But later. Do you want me to stay with you for a while?"

He took her hand and gave it a quick, light squeeze. "No," he said, "I know there's plenty to do. Just leave me some water, and don't let me sleep through lunch."

Giesla returned the pressure of his hand and said, "Yes, you probably will sleep some more. Here are two canteens, and there is consommé in the vacuum bottle." She pointed to a steel thermos on the stone floor beside her.

Tag said to Giesla as she left, "Tell the gang I'm doing fine."

When she had gone, Tag drank a half canteen of water and some of the beef tea and dozed again. He awoke to the smell of pot roast.

Someone had knocked together an invalid's table out of old ammo boxes, and Giesla was putting it across his lap. On it were two mess-kit halves full of roast, potatoes, and cabbage, and a large bottle cap full of an assortment of pills. Colonel Barlow stood at the end of the cot.

"Feeling hungry, Max?" he said.

Tag rolled to his left and pushed himself up into a sitting position. He felt dizzy, a little feverish, but he did have an appetite.

"Sharp set," Tag said.

"If you are hungry, the doctor said you should eat," Giesla said. "But first we must measure your temperature." She took a digital thermometer from the breast pocket of her jumpsuit, reset it, and slipped it under Tag's tongue.

"Max," Colonel Barlow went on, "I know you're anxious to know what the story is from SACEUR, so if you feel up to it, I'll fill you in while you eat."

Giesla removed the thermometer, and Tag said, "Thanks, I'd appreciate it. The doctor, Harrison, he said I'd be staying in the field, right?"

Barlow nodded and pulled up an ammunition box to the side of the cot. "That's right," he said. "Go ahead and eat, Max. I'll give you the whole skinny."

"Gentlemen," Giesla said, "I have some interrogations. So, if you will excuse me . . . ?"

"Of course," Barlow said, "and thank you."

He turned back to Tag, who was chewing slowly, savoring the scrounged roast, not even considering where it came from. "Well," Barlow began, "things are still happening awfully fast, Max—that is, where they haven't come to a complete stop. I don't know how much you recall of our conversation when you were first brought in, but not a lot has changed on the map since then. We've broken the Soviet line at Fulda; the Warsaw Pact army in the north has been halted and, in places, pushed back. The situation up there is just about a wash. Between here and Fulda, we've moved their line back nearly to Mannheim. All that is good, and the cease-fire seems to be holding up. The problem is still this damned First Guards Army."

Tag looked at him quizzically, a lump of unchewed beef bulging in his jaw.

"I know," Barlow went on. "I told you that you had scratched their plans to break out—and you did—but the problem, officially, is political not military. From where we stand right here, we see a Soviet army in a bottle. They have the French in their faces in the Black Forest, their backs to Lake Constance, and a twenty-kilometer wide strip of hot fallout between them and us. Kettle has found us some more units to fill in the line down here, and we'd be no match for the First Guards on a level field. Luckily, that hot margin makes it impossible for them to get out without exposing a long flank. They've got to stay put, fight, or starve, and Kettle would like to see all three. That's the rub."

"So SACEUR still has a hard-on for the First Guards, huh?" Tag asked.

Barlow nodded. "It *was* the First Guards who actually launched the atomic exchange. That's a bee the general hasn't been able to get out of his bonnet. When he contacted the Soviet general staff immediately after our counterstrike, he specifically excluded the First Guards from the units he would allow to withdraw under a cease-fire. The Soviets were anxious to get the nukes off the field, and I suppose they thought that was important enough for them to go along, thinking the First Guards' situation could be negotiated later. But Kettle's intent was to single the First Guards out for punishment, and he hasn't backed down an inch.

"I was with him, Max, when the exchange took place, and I thought the man was going to be physically ill. It broke his heart. To him, it was a breach of humanity, an opening of Pandora's box, and it forced him to do something that was entirely abhorrent to him. The politicians, once they took over the negotiations from the generals, kept him from publicly pinning the blame on the Soviet leaders, so he laid it at the feet of the First Guards. He has sound military objections against letting them out, and he's done too damn well otherwise for Washington to relieve him of command—hell, all NATO would revolt—so SACEUR is facing a standoff on each side, against his enemy's army and against his government's policy. So far, he's standing up on both fronts."

"How so?" Tag mumbled through a mouthful of potatoes.

"In all, the cease-fire is better for us than it is for Ivan. We have more resources, and now we have time to bring them across the pond. The Soviets have already put everything they have in the field, and it took a pounding. So, Kettle's military position has never been stronger. And as long as he can produce convincing military reasons for keeping the First Guards bottled up and keeps out of the direct political negotiations, Washington won't cross him. And Kettle knows this. He's read his Clausewitz, and he knows the value of war as 'continuation of policy by other means.' And Washington's policy—or at least *position*—is that we've won, won't give an inch and want a whole lot back. But the White House seems to be nervous, too, because of some mixed signals we've been getting concerning the infighting in the Kremlin."

Tag arched his brows over a forkful of cabbage.

Barlow allowed himself the knowing smile of an officer on the general's staff. "You'd be surprised," he said, "how good our intelligence is inside the politburo, Max. There are still enough disgruntled holdovers from the Gorbachev and Svetlov years to make moles easy. Still, the way the new party is compartmentalized, there's probably only a couple of dozen who really know which way the wind is blowing across Red Square. The official communiqués are still pretty tough, but we're getting word of food riots, antiwar riots, even anti-Party riots from all over. Two of the top three leaders haven't been seen or heard in days, and nearly a hundred chairs were empty at the Supreme Soviet all week. Washington won't push things until they know who they're dealing with, and we're left in limbo down here, fighting a nonwar, invisible as long as the cease-fire is in effect."

Tag swallowed and sucked his teeth. "Okay," he said, "I think I'm getting all this, Colonel. Do we have any new orders?"

"Yes and no, Max. Your gee-two from the last foray and the latest satellite info indicate that the First Guards are pulling back inside their perimeter. They've called in their recon teams and armored foragers—no penetrations along the nuclear zone—so

we don't have anything immediately on tap. But—
and this is a big but, Max—Kettle is convinced that
they're up to something. He wants us here in case they
are. We still have a confused situation down here in
SOUTHAG. We're pretty sure there is some Soviet
armor left in the Jura, between here and the Black
Forest, maybe even isolated by the nukes, probably
out of communication with their command. Kettle
wants them found, captured if possible."

Tag wiped his mouth with the back of his hand.
"There are better places to be, if we do have a fast-
reaction call," he said.

Barlow's dark face broke into another delighted
smile. "You're getting way ahead of yourself, Max,"
he said. "Everything that's happened—the nuclear
exchange, the Soviet political uncertainties, the shaky
nature of this cease-fire—has had everyone over-
reacting. We think now that Ivan wants to observe the
cease-fire very closely for a while, lick his wounds, and
look for an opening, maybe try some sort of political
maneuver to get Kettle out of the way. We, meanwhile,
are going to do much the same. But we're also going to
clean up a few loose ends, consolidate our forces, and
establish our areas of control. You're going to have
a couple of weeks off at least, while our Special Ops
teams try to locate those strays I mentioned. Between
the hits you and the tank took, we're damn lucky to
be able to get parts for the both of you."

Tag's shoulder felt tight and hot, and he was heavy
with his meal. "Okay, Colonel," he said. "I'll see the
crew after I've had a little nap."

Colonel Barlow sat Tag's lap table beside the cot,
and Tag was snoring softly by the time Barlow was
out from under the canopy.

Tag was in some pain when Bones came in later

to give him another hypo, but he felt better when he awoke at 1800 hours and found Giesla, Lt. Prentice, Fruits Tutti, and Ham Jefferson standing by his cot. The doctor, Captain Harrison, was kneeling beside Tag, lifting the bandage to examine the wound.

"Feel up to some company?" Harrison asked.

"Yeah," Tag said sleepily. "I guess so. Who are these people, anyway?"

"Shit," Ham Jefferson said, "ain't nothing wrong with him, is they, Fruit Loops?"

"Naw," said Tutti. "When youse makes a silk-purse officer outta a sow's-ear sergeant, deys always some memory loss. It's just natural."

"Thanks," Tag said. "I didn't know you cared." He turned to look at Harrison. "How's it look, Bill?"

"Oh, something between pounded steak and ground round. You're going to heal fine, Max. You must have one hell of an immune system. I just wanted to check the sutures and have a look at you before I said okay to a house party of wild commandos. I'm going to have Bones rig you up an IV drip of antibiotics, so you can sleep through later."

Tag nodded and said to the others, "Before we start socializing, pull up some ammo crates and give me a sitrep."

Harrison nodded his assent behind Tag's back, and they found places to sit.

"An hour, no more," the doctor said as he packed to leave. "But no booze and no dancing."

Giesla helped Tag prop himself up with a duffel bag and a pillow, and he said to Prentice, "Chuck, you first. What's the skinny on the Bradleys and our Rangers?"

Prentice bugged his eyes. "And how are you?" he said. "I'm fine, thanks."

Tag grinned back at him. "Right," he said. "That's what I meant to say. Go on, Chuck."

"The men are okay, Max," said Prentice. "We had a couple of them get banged around, but no dead and no one seriously injured. The Bradleys are another story. Mine took one bad shot, you probably recall, and it has all sorts of problems—lost the antenna array and one missile rack, screwed up a hatch, and jammed one of the coax machine guns. N. Sain's machine fared better, but it was contaminated worse. The NBC guys are still steaming it off."

"Can your track be fixed?" Tag asked.

"Logistics Support Group is supposed to be dropping in parts and technicians, so I guess they think they can repair it in the field."

Tag faced Ham Jefferson. "Ham," he said, "the same true for us?"

Ham nodded, uneasy with having to talk about the damage that had killed the driver of the No Slack Too and given Tag his wound. "Just a hatch replacement, bossman, and a few readouts on the console. But we're quarantined right now, until the NBC crew gets finished. We were real dirty, man."

"Did you get the videotapes, the ones we took coming out?"

"Copied, edited, and ever'thing," Fruits said. "Soon as I can get back in the tank, I'll make copies onta discs for you."

"Kettle has his?" Tag asked.

"Captain," Ham said reassuringly, "we've dotted all the eyes and crossed all the tees. I wrote up the preliminary report, and Lieutenant Prentice countersigned it, and Colonel Barlow has been over it with us twice."

"So, you know our orders."

"No, Max," said Giesla. "The colonel said you would know those."

Tag nodded and explained his conversation with Barlow. "So," he concluded, "enjoy it while you can, and keep me posted on any rumors you hear, especially if any of those people we contacted inside the zone decide to come out, Soviets or civilians. Any new business?"

"Just that N. Sain wants to see you," Prentice said.

"About what?" Tag asked. "Why didn't he come in with all of you?"

Prentice shrugged. "He didn't say he had to be alone with you. He just wanted to be sure it was okay."

"You never know what to expect from that guy," Tag said. "Sure, bring him in."

With that, the flap of the canopy parted and in stepped Sergeant M. N. Sain, the Rommel of rock 'n' roll, a deranged reservist who had been caught up in World War Three while on USO tour to visit his two sidemen who had enlisted in lieu of going to jail for drug infractions. Now here he stood, boots unlaced, trousers unbloused, shirtless, unshaven, sweating and smiling and holding a gut-string acoustic guitar.

"O Avatar of Ambush," N. Sain said, shifting from foot to foot, acting anxious as a dog about to go for a walk, "the dark oneness cannot yet contain your essence, your perfect harmonic. The beast has bitten you and dragged you 'round, but you brought it home at last, back to the belly of the earth, stone womb of our mother. Something soft to soothe the beast."

N. Sain held the guitar like a ham on display, smiled, and lost the focus in one eye.

"Sure," Tag said. "But only in the Apollonian mode, my Dark Disciple."

N. Sain sat on a box at the foot of the cot, facing away from the rest, and began to tune the guitar by half tones.

"We thought for a wake, we ought to have some music," Ham said. "Sorry you can't have a drink, bossman." He pulled a full bottle of sour-mash whiskey out of the gas-mask bag at his waist.

Tag reached out and took the bottle by the neck. "Just a small one for luck," he said.

Ham let go of the bottle. Tag worried out the cork with his teeth, spat it in his lap, and raised the whiskey. "To our friend and comrade in arms, Robert Edward Lee Latta. Wheels, I hope the whiskey in heaven is all twenty years old, the revenuers slow, and the women fast. And I hope they don't keep you out for lying."

Tag threw back his head and took a long, reckless pull on the neck of the bottle, the whiskey searing hot in his throat. He snapped his head forward, gagged, and spewed liquor, glad that his coughing and choking disguised his tears.

Giesla leapt to his side to pat his back, and Ham grabbed the bottle.

"Damn," the gunner said. "Rank ain't got the privilege of wastin' good whiskey, bossman."

"Drink," Tag croaked. Giesla slapped his back, and Tag belched.

"Wheels," Ham said, looking up at the peak of the canopy, "you're an original, son. As bad color-blind as you were a cracker. A fearless motherfucker. A good friend and a good soldier." He drank and passed the bottle to Fruits.

"Wheels, ya rube," the loader said, "if I knows youse, you're pullin' double duty right now. Heaven for you will be sittin' aroun' and tellin' stories, and hell will be ever'body else havin' to listen to them."

When the bottle had passed to Giesla and Prentice and back to Tag, he let it go by, and N. Sain said over his shoulder, "This is for the one who's gone full circle, O Avatar."

Everyone stopped to look at N. Sain, who sat with his hairy back hunched toward them. His left hand touched the neck of the guitar, slid down it once, and pure soft notes began to pour from the instrument, like circles of crystallized smoke that evaporated into the parachute silk, at once definite and ephemeral, full of clarity and emotion. The tune was "Whiskey River."

As he listened, Tag was touched by the simple, plaintive music, but even more was stunned by N. Sain through the music. This side of him Tag had never seen, for there was no disguising in the melody a tenderness and depth of feeling that all of N. Sain's previous behavior would deny. It was nothing like the frenetic rock or strutting soul he had heard N. Sain listen to and play before. When the song ended, N. Sain began another at once, this time "Here Comes the Sun."

N. Sain played, and Giesla, Prentice, Ham, and Fruits emptied the bottle, while Tag told story after story about Wheels Latta. Then everyone left, and Tag slept again until morning.

Dr. Harrison had been right, and Tag was fast to mend. Within three days he was up and walking, off the stronger painkillers. After ten days he was regaining some mobility in the shoulder and put himself back on full duty, which was light enough. Nothing had changed significantly since Tag first came in wounded—there were no changes in orders from General Kettle—and the parts and technicians to fix Prentice's Bradley and the No Slack Too had just arrived. At the end of three weeks, with the repairs almost complete and an ominous silence from SACEUR hanging in the air, Tag felt well enough to walk with Giesla on a picnic up the mountain above the mineworks.

They chose a gentle slope and walked it for most of an hour, Giesla leading with their food in a rucksack on her back, until they came to a meadow no larger than a lawn, surrounded by beech trees. Near its center was a spring that welled into a stone-lined pool.

Tag unslung the blanket he had tied over his shoulder and spread it by the pool, using his stiff right arm clumsily. The bruise and swelling had gone down, and the scar tissue would not be deep, but his shoulder was still sore as hell.

Giesla had dropped her rucksack and taken off her boots and was sitting with her feet in the water.

"Come cool your feet, soldier," she said.

He sat beside her, and she helped him with his laces. Tag rolled up his cuffs, slid his feet into the water that was warm only at the very top, and lay back beside Giesla, looking at the sky through the ring of beeches.

After a while, Giesla said, without turning her head, "I wish this could be our whole world, Max: water, meadow, trees, and the sun in a blue sky."

"It is our world right now, Gies," said Tag. "Our world within a world. It's here for us, for right now, but it would be too lonely to live in, too lonely and too selfish."

"Someday, though," she said. "Someday it will not be. We will put an end to this war and come back here. Duty has saved me, Max, saved me from grief about my husband, my brother, my friends who have died. But it is becoming like a drug, and I need to be off it, if only for a little while."

"I know," he said. "It's the thing bigger than our-selves that we've both used to see us through. But I don't think it's going to go on much longer, Gies. I really don't. Nobody is going to want to crank up the big guns again."

Giesla rolled on one elbow and looked down into Tag's face. "And I believe you," she said, "but that is all in another world—*ja?* In this world there is only one big gun." She ran her hand hard down his thigh.

"You," he said, "are an evil woman, but I know you won't take advantage of a cripple."

"Silly boy," Giesla said. She bit him on the lower lip and began to unzip his jumpsuit.

When they were both naked and spent and she lay on top of him taking her breaths in tiny gasps, a single cloud passed across the sun, chilling them, and Giesla rose, commanding Tag to lie still while she fixed them lunch. They ate, splashed in the cold spring, dressed, and walked back down the mountain, back to the world.

Prentice was waiting at the wire around the perim-eter.

"Max," he said, "Colonel Barlow wants to see you. I think it's orders from SACEUR."

The world had come to meet them.

2

After the desultory pace of the past four weeks, Tag felt the swell of events as a physical presence. The Early Bird satellite photos had shown movement out from the Soviet concentration, a single column striking north toward the Jura and several units dispersing west, in the direction of the Black Forest. Almost at once, a Special Ops team operating in the Jura had notified Barlow that they had located one of the lost Soviet tank detachments. The three T-80s and two BMPs were no more than thirty kilometers from the mineworks, but across the band of nuclear destruction that marked the old Soviet line, where missile launchers disguised as artillery and armor had been laid in ambush for an entire NATO army.

"Max," Barlow said as Tag signaled the Rangers into the Bradleys, "we can get you another driver from division. I can have him here today."

"No time, sir," Tag said. "The No Slack Too takes a while to learn."

"You sure you can handle it yourself, with that shoulder?"

Tag grinned at him. "I can't scratch behind my ear, but I can still reach the steering yokes. If I didn't think I could, I wouldn't risk my people's lives, Colonel. Not for this."

"Good hunting, Max," Barlow said.

Tag bent an awkward salute with his stiff arm, then turned and scrambled over the side of the XM-F4 tank and into the commander's hatch. He clapped a CVC on his head and spoke over the tactical radio frequency: "Okay, you meat eaters, this is Butcher Boy. Let's go take some hides."

Tag's command roared to life. Giesla's three commando cars, with their bristling pods of 106mm recoilless rifles on either side, missile racks on top, and miniguns on the nose, slapped the air with their exhaust as they moved in low gear through the gap in the perimeter and spread out in echelon in the big woods beyond. Tag and his crew followed in the No Slack Too, and the hyper-Bradleys came behind them, fanning out on the flanks.

Tag had watched over the repair and refitting of his tank and Prentice's Bradley with special care. He no longer felt invulnerable inside the slick-skin armor, and while he was recovering his strength he spent hours lurking over the shoulders of the mechanics and technicians. It had reminded him again of how much they all missed Wheels Latta, whose knack with everything mechanical had saved their butts more than once. But it also helped him focus his thoughts on something other than Wheels, and he felt now that he knew his armor better than ever before. Under the eye of the technicians, Tag had allowed Fruits Tutti to tinker with the closed-loop radar on the Phalanx system, so that now their 37mm air-defense and light antiarmor weapon could pick out something as small as a man in an open field. A software link with the LandNav system had enhanced their indirect-fire accuracy, and a resupply of War Club missiles had provided them with a generation said to be proof against all Soviet jamming techniques and also have ground-to-ground capabilities superior to Ivan's tube-fired Songsters and Tree Toads. The Bradleys both had new gusset plates where their monopolar carbide noses and sides joined the conventional armor plating, and both the Bradleys and the XM-F4 had been refit-ted with several NBC defense innovations, including new seals, filters, and internal oxygen supplies. Tag felt the immense emptiness of Wheels Latta's chair beside him, but he felt no self-pity now. Now, he had a duty, and he had to drive.

He hadn't lost his touch. Tag rode with his chair elevated, so he could keep his head outside the hatch, and steered by feel. Fruits Tutti rode in the driver's seat, where he could still command the Phalanx, and kept an eye on the instruments and screens, while Ham remained in the turret, at the trigger of the 120mm main gun.

It was full autumn now in the Jura, the broad stands of hardwoods aflame with color, the giant evergreens brilliant against that backdrop. The air was cold and mountain-dry, but the sun still rode high enough to be warm on Tag's face as he navigated them south-east, down the spine of the mountains. This was familiar territory to him now. They had fought for it, and now they owned it. Oddly, it was what lay behind their lines that menaced them—that and the line itself. Already the radiation sensors on the No Slack Too were beginning to respond—Tutti called up their status every few minutes—and Tag knew it was time for him to pull his head in and look again at the updated maps. Ground recon had given them a fairly accurate idea of where they could enter the radioactive swath in relative safety, but not even the aircraft photos and RAD readings were much help once they were inside. Still, Tag thought as he eased down the hydraulic pedestal of his seat, it was a narrow band they had to cross, and they could do it fast.

When the radiation counter reached the high end of normal range, Tag switched on the TacNet and ordered everyone to halt and button up. While the others were stopped, he moved the No Slack Too forward to lead the infiltration across the atomic waste.

Coming up on it was like approaching the scene of a great forest fire. First there were trees with withered tops, then ones that were scorched, and finally blackened skeletons of timber began to appear, and the undergrowth was carbonized. Then, even the remains of standing trees were gone, and the raider party was moving over an area burned clean, with only the occasional carcass of a truck or artillery piece or launch platform to testify to what had happened here. The line had been saturated by explosive nukes, whose radioactivity had a shorter half-life than that of the neutron warheads. So, while there was no getting around the tactical radii of the impacts, there were paths of temperate radiation through the scatter of ground-zero points.

Their traverse took the raiders across a narrow waist in the line, no more than five kilometers wide, but it was enough to remind them all of what had happened and what the world, through them, had narrowly escaped. The spikes on the radiation sensors jumped like mad things, and in the heart of the strike zone was a concentration of the reason for the carnage. The blackened and twisted frames of a half-dozen mobile missile launchers were strung off to Tag's right, and on the ground around them were charred grotesques that it took him a moment to recognize as the bodies of Soviet soldiers. Some of them were only an arm or a leg bent in an impossible contortion, their bodies reduced to ash, powdered shadow. Tag shuddered and picked up speed.

Because of the prevailing winds on the day of the atomic attack, fallout had spread the hot margin of the zone deeper into the forest on its southwest side, so it was nearly a half hour after they had made their crossing before Tag could signal a stand-down from NBC defenses and, since they were keeping radio silence, call a quick conference.

Prentice, his topkick Krager and the Ranger squad leaders, Dunn and Villalobos, joined Tag and Giesla at N. Sain's Bradley.

"Okay," Tag said, "we're on unfamiliar ground now, so let's keep things tight. We're about ten klicks from where the Special Ops team is supposed to link up with us, and about fifteen from the last reported position of the Soviet strays. Now, the green beanies may not be at the rendezvous to meet us, so we'll take up a perimeter at once. I want the Rangers out of the Bradleys and on the ground immediately. Chuck, N. Sain, you key off me. The No Slack Too will be the twelve o'clock. Chuck, you take four, and N. Sain, eight. Giesla, you and your gun buggies fill in the gaps. There's not a lot we can do until we get the detailed gee-two from our guys on the ground. Any questions?"

"Sir," Villalobos said, "is there any sort of pass-word or sign so we'll know if it's the Special Ops guys coming in?"

"Don't worry," Tag said, "you'll recognize 'em. They'll be the ones in green. Let's go. Giesla, take the point. The coordinates are there on your map."

The crest of the mountains rose steadily as the raiders moved southwest, toward the twin headwaters of the Danube and the Neckar at the edge of the Black Forest and in the heart of Germany's highest mountains outside the Bavarian Alps. The forest was huge here and old. Stands of larch and fir domi-nated the thinning hardwoods, and there were easy avenues among the ancient trunks for a column of light armor. Giesla had them at the rendezvous with-in thirty minutes, and they set their perimeter in the midafternoon.

After completing his inspection of the perimeter, satisfied that his men had lost none of their edge, Tag was sitting in the shade of the No Slack Too's camouflage net, going over the topo maps of the area, when one of the Rangers came with word that the Special Forces team was approaching the perimeter.

"Okay," said Tag, rising and brushing the leaves from his seat, "bring them over here when they get inside. And tell Lieutenant Prentice and Lieutenant Ruther to join us."

The four-man Special Operations team came sloping through the trees, all in camouflage and hung with exotic field gear, like warriors from a science-fiction novel. Each man carried, in addition to a full-automatic 7.62mm carbine and an assortment of speciality gre-nades, two of the latest generation LAWs, a miniature microwave radio, and a bulging "booby hatch"—a pouch containing the makings for a variety of booby traps, including remote laser-activated fuses and canisters of debilitating gas. The man in the lead came up to Tag and said, "Butcher Boy? I'm Wily Coyote, C. B. Randall."

Tag took the man's hand. "Max Tag," he said. "Drop you gear. You all want some chow? I've got a German ham and some black bread stashed in the turret."

The lanky Special Forces officer flashed a boyish, incongruous smile. "Sounds good," he said, "but let's cut the cheese first. We may want to move before dark."

When Prentice and Giesla had joined them, Randall squatted over Tag's map and outlined the situation.

"There are three T-80s and two BMPs in the element we have located, about here" —he tapped the acetate-covered map with a twig— "and they're not likely to move. The BMPs are in AT configuration, with just the crews on board, no troops. We've been trailing them for two days, and they've got to be about out of fuel. As you can see, they have invested this piece of high ground, and it's a good position. There's only one approach armor can make on it, up this down-slope ridge, and any fighting positions on the mountain above them are screened by the forest. You'd have to be within two or three hundred meters to get a clear shot. For their part, they've got good fields of fire, good cover among some rock outcrops. Food and fuel is where they're hurting."

"Okay, Randall," said Tag, "you've actually seen the place, and we haven't. You have any ideas on how to take them?"

"If it was just a matter of taking them out," the

Green Beret replied, "no problem. But if we want prisoners, it's a little trickier. One, we could just ask them to surrender. Two, we could slip in and make a snatch. Or three, we could try to get them off that rise and into the woods, disable the vehicles, and scoop 'em all up as they came out."

"Is your gee-two good enough to know who to snatch?" Tag asked.

Randall shrugged. "We've identified the commanders, but I don't know which one's the big enchilada. One of the T-80 commanders probably, but we just don't know."

"Never mind," Tag said. "We've got to neutralize them anyway. We can't leave the rest of them running loose, even if we get the prisoners. Any radio traffic to or from them?"

"Yesterday," Randall said, "just before they took up their position, there were a couple of satellite burps in and out, but nothing we could unscramble with our field gear."

Everyone was silent a moment while Tag chewed his cheek in thought. At last Giesla said, "I think we must move at once, Max, and use Captain Randall's third option. With our foot troops and mobility, we can take them in the forest."

Tag looked at the faces around him. "Anybody have a better idea?" he asked. When no one answered, he said, "Okay, then. Let's make a plan and break camp. Hey, Fruits," Tag called toward the turret of the XM-F4, "whip up some sandwiches and get us ready to roll."

Captain Randall rode with Tag to within a kilometer of the Soviet position, then he, his team, and the Rangers in the Bradleys dismounted to set their ambushes and blocking forces in the woods along with Giesla's

Jagd Kommandos, while the No Slack Too and the APCs maneuvered up-slope, scouting for firing positions among the dense timber and rocky outcrops of the Swabian Jura.

The knoll occupied by the Soviets was small, with steep walls on the up-slope side and wide washes separating it from the bulk of the mountain. The best Tag could do for his primary position was a spot roughly even with the top of the knoll and three hundred meters away across one of the washes. He had the concealment of some fallen timber, but no cover worth the name, and he could command less than half of the knoll with his main gun. Still, it would have to do. He hoped Prentice and N. Sain were able to cover the rest. After jockeying slowly into place, running the tank on whisper mode, he scanned the knoll for nearly a half hour through his commander's scope, observing movement and marking targets for his gunner.

The Soviet armor was all unbuttoned, hatches thrown wide, and one or two men were outside each of the vehicles that he could see, smoking and eating. An hour before sunset, he gave the order: "Fruits, load gas and bring up two smoke rounds to follow. Ham, put the gas in the big middle of all of them, then bounce those smoke rounds off the T-80 and the BMP nearest us. We'll scoot then, and I want a sabot in the tube when we do. Mark one."

"Confirmed," the gunner replied as the loading carousel spun and seated a CS gas round in the breech.

"Shoot."

"Shot."

"Fire two at will."

The shell containing the smothering gas exploded

before the muzzle report had brought the Soviet soldiers to their feet. Their shouts of panic and confusion were muffled by the smoke rounds striking in rapid succession, the first engulfing one of the T-80s and the second smothering a BMP, whose tracks separated from their carriage with the impact. In less than a minute, before the Soviet gunners could draw a bead, the entire top of the knoll was wreathed in thick smoke and choking gas. In that minute, Tag had revved up the turbines and raced to his secondary position, one hundred meters to his left.

Blips lit on the heat-detection screens of the No Slack Too as the Soviet engines coughed to life, and Tag could follow them as well on the closed-loop screen of the Phalanx. His secondary position offered him an even smaller field of fire—he was sighting from between the trunks of two enormous trees—but his angle was better.

"Fruits," he said to the loader, "take the Phalanx on manual and dust 'em up a little."

Fruits rotated his seat to the Phalanx console, threw a toggle to release the radar lock, and hosed the hill with 37mm depleted-uranium slugs that exploded on impact with the trees and rocks around the rim, setting up a hellish cacophony that spurred the Communist tanks into movement.

"Ceasefire, Fruits," Tag ordered. "You've got 'em stirring now."

Suddenly a missile hurled from the fog of smoke, dragging it like a contrail behind, and struck the bole of the tree three feet to the right of the No Slack Too. Its detonation shattered the trunk, which burst into flame and crashed down across the rear deck of the XM-F4, jolting the men inside.

Tag had no choice but to gun the turbines. The

powerful engines strained to come out from under the weight. He locked alternate tracks to throw off the tree, ground forward until one tread caught the burning stump, and the No Slack Too heaved up on that side, fought out from under its load, and broke free with a lurch.

"Target, Bossman," Ham called over the intercom.

"Take the sonofabitch," Tag said, still fighting the controls with his bad arm and looking for where he wanted to go.

"Shot," Ham said as he released the integral-propellant sabot from the tube. It sliced through the smoke and found the crippled BMP that had fired on them. It came apart like a sprung watch, the violence of the explosion sending hatches and buckled plates of armor spinning up out of the smoke.

"They're runnin'," Ham said, "scramblin' like ants. Man, this heat screen is goin' wild."

"Ham," said Tag, "are they abandoning or redeploying?"

"They haulin' ass."

"Okay. Hang on for bumps."

Tag aimed the No Slack Too down the slope, flying over the rough spots and juking between the trees. He would take them all the way to the bottom of the wash and run it around the base of the knoll, to where the Soviets would have to debouch, then fall in from behind to cover the men on the ground.

The Rangers were ready for the pell-mell file of Soviet armor that poured off the knoll and down the slim finger of a ridge to the north. Only the lead T-80 escaped the salvo from their LAWs that ripped off tracks and punctured the ventilator grilles of the remaining BMP and the other two tanks. The lead tank absorbed two glancing hits on its flanks, but sped on unimpeded, crashing through the undergrowth like a wounded boar.

Mathias Betcher, the senior NCO of the Jagd Kommandos, had hunted boar in these mountains before, and he knew how easy it was to outwit a frightened pig. As he and the other Kommandos had moved their gun buggies into position, he had noted the wet-weather stream that looped down the mountain, how it made a broad bend around a rise, where the timber thinned. Now, as the snarling T-80 plunged into the timber and out of everyone's field of fire, Betcher turned to his driver, Karl, and ordered him into the woods. Karl protested that the course would take them away from the fleeing tank, and Betcher told him, "Drive."

As Karl careened through the woods, spinning forest mulch from beneath the honeycomb tires of the commando car, the Rangers were closing in on the three pieces of disabled armor, none of which were yet ready to give up the fight.

The BMP had begun slinging 73mm rounds from its turret cannon almost as soon as the LAWs hit it. Although it filled the forest with concussions and shrapnel, it hit no one, but trying to rush the APC on foot was too risky, especially with its nose-mounted machine gun still operable. One of the stranded T-80s was in much the same shape, but the other had taken a rocket through its rear grille that destroyed the motor and ignited a fire that had driven the crew out of the hatches. The commander still stood in the turret hatch, covering his men with the 12.7mm machine gun mounted on top. The Rangers were sticking to their orders, laying down only light suppressing fire and changing positions after each burst, trying to avoid casualties on both sides.

That was the situation when Tag and the No Slack Too rounded the base of the knoll and came in sight of the Soviet vehicles. They were no more than a hundred meters from the BMP, and Tag had a clear alley to it through the trees. His first instinct was to call for a shot, but he did not know where the Rangers were in relation to the BMP, only that they were close.

"Gentlemen," he said to his crew, "stand by to ram."

With that, he brought the XM-F4 on line with the Soviet APC, opened the throttles on both turbines, and dropped the transmission into a lower gear. The No Slack Too accelerated with g-force speed, slamming Tag back in his seat as it rose on its air-torsion suspension, tracks spinning, and flew across the hundred meters in less than four seconds, sending thirty low-slung tons of fighting machine full-tilt into the rear quarter panel of the BMP. The lighter piece of armor went airborne from the collision, and the No Slack Too hardly slowed. It struck the BMP again just as it hit the ground, this time bowling it over on one side, its armor crumpled like foil.

The two T-80s in front of the BMP had registered with Tag even as he made the dash, and he immediately ordered Ham to lay the main gun on them. As the turret came around, Tag saw the horrified Soviet tank commander standing at the machine gun in the next turret ahead. He flipped on the exterior loudspeaker of the XM-F4 and said, "Give it up, Ivan."

The man threw up his hands and climbed awkwardly out of the hatch and down the side of the tank.

Distracted by the small-arms fire from the Rangers, the other disabled tank was not aware of what had happened behind it. Its commander and crew had no time to consider, however, when Sgt. Dunn came up from behind, leapt onto the rear deck, and dropped a CS grenade down the breathing snorkel. All they had time to think of was how fast they could get out, only too happy to surrender to the lone sergeant who greeted them.

Prentice's Bradley appeared from the other side of the knoll, and the remainder of the Rangers swarmed over the Soviet prisoners and their vehicles. Tag negotiated around the tanks and found Krager taking charge of rounding up the prisoners.

"Gaylord," Tag said, "what happened to the third tank?"

"The sonofabitch got past us, Max," the first sergeant said. "But I think I saw Betcher take off after it."

"Which way?" Tag asked, readying himself for the chase.

Krager turned to point, opened his mouth to speak, and was stopped by the whoosing report of a 106mm recoilless rifle and the ringing detonation of a high-explosive round.

Krager dropped his hand. "About over there, I'd say."

Tag smiled wryly. "Yeah, thanks, Gaylord," he said. "You have anybody back on the knoll looking for stay-behinds?"

"Your Sergeant Dunn and four men. I think the green beanies may have gone with them."

"Good. Let's get this place policed up and get the hell out of here. Make sure you don't miss any papers inside these vehicles."

Krager shook his head. "Lord, Lord," he said. "How have I survived all these years without you?"

Tag maneuvered the No Slack Too past the last tank and through the forest in the direction of the cannon fire he had heard. He found Betcher's vehicle on a low bank above the water course, where the remaining T-80 sat with a gaping hole in its rear deck from the shot Betcher had delivered from above. The shaken tank crew were lined up in front of it, being frisked by two other of Giesla's men, while Betcher looked on, grinning his bearish grin.

"Mathias," Tag shouted down from the bank, "look for anything you can find inside and wait here. I'll send one of the Bradleys for the prisoners. We're moving out of here."

Betcher waved at him, barked something in German, and then shouted back to Tag, "Now *this* is Kommando war, Herr Captain. At this we are good."

Twenty minutes later Tag was leading his column higher up the Jura through the lengthening shadows of evening. He halted them a half hour before sunset and set positions in a copse of beeches near the crest. He was feeling good. He had been able to function with his gimpy shoulder. They had accomplished their mission and taken no casualties. It was a good day's work.

Once the watches were set and the men all fed, Tag assembled his command group and had the prisoners brought out of the Bradleys for interrogation. There were fifteen captured Soviets in all, including one in his forties who wore no insignia but had the bearing of someone in command. Giesla had already been over the log books and papers taken from them, enough so, at least, that she already knew the answers to the standard questions about their unit and movements in the past few weeks.

"So," she said in Russian to the rankless prisoner, "I see you have been in contact with First Guards' command. You do not really think that they can help, do you?"

The man said nothing. He stood with his hands tied behind him in the circle of Allies and stared at them with the look of a shackled wolf, angry and defiant.

Ham Jefferson, who had often helped Giesla with her interrogations, stepped forward and said, "You want me to cut his balls off, Gies?"

"Please," she said sharply, frustrated by the Russian's intransigence.

Ham's hand-honed Lile knife appeared in his hand.

"You will not let that black African ape touch me," said the prisoner in perfect, only slightly accented English.

"Touch you?" said Tag in mock incredulity. "Goodness no, Ivan. He wouldn't touch white meat with his hand. Would you, Hambone."

"Gracious, no," Ham said, advancing with the knife held low. "That's what they makes knives for." He slipped the blade beneath the Russian's web belt and cut through it effortlessly, then sliced loose the top button of his trousers.

"This is against the Geneva accords," the man said, his eyes growing wider. "You cannot torture me."

"Won't be no torture, Ivan," Ham said sweetly. "You just gonna die slow, that's all." He separated the next button from the man's fly.

"Chesnokov," the man blurted. "Ivan Chesnokov. Yes, my name is Ivan. I am artillery major, not with these others. I know nothing of what they do. We have been cut off many weeks."

Ham stepped away and said to Giesla, "Isn't it amazing how well that always works?"

"You are an artist, Mr. Jefferson," she said.

Giesla continued to question the prisoners for three hours before she was satisfied they had told her all she could get from them that night.

"Okay," Tag said at last. "Chuck, I want you to get a couple hours of rack, then take these guys back to Barlow. The Special Ops people say there's a small town about twenty klicks south of here that needs some checking out. You can meet us there when you come back. You folks have all done good work today. I get the feeling that we're about to wrap this war up."

3

Despite his optimism of the night before, Tag awoke anxious in the small hours before dawn. The previous day's exertions had been hard on his shoulder, and its ache only added to his feeling of unease. It was something more than just his lingering grief over Wheels's death. It was a feeling that he had forgotten something important, overlooked some critical detail in his flush of accomplishment following the defeat of the Soviet armor. He lay on his back on his inflatable bedroll, staring at the stars and worrying his memory, trying to train it on real things and ignore the bugbears of imagination.

One supposition, however, he could not deny. With winter coming on, the First Guards Army was not going to be content to starve. Barlow's contention that General Kettle would accept that fate for them did not ring true. SACEUR was not passive in his will. More likely, Tag thought, Kettle was counting on the First Guards' predicament to goad them into a fight. And the tighter the circle around them, the more likely that became. Moreover, Tag was the knot on the noose, drawing it closer with each foray, provoking the cornered Soviets with his every move. And, he realized, they knew him now. The No Slack Too and his mixed bag of Rangers were no longer an element of surprise, and there were too few of them. He wondered, if they were all that stood between Ivan and a breakout, how thin the Allies were stretched across Germany.

Tag sat up, opened a canteen beside him, and splashed his face with water. Then, it hit him, the thing that had been nagging his memory. He knew from Randall, the Special Ops team leader, that the Soviet tankers they had captured sent and received a message burp before taking the positions where Tag and his raiders hit them. But had they had a chance to send another during the confusion of the fight? They still had the capability, and no one had been monitoring to check. Too late now. Prentice was halfway to Barlow with them by now, and Tag was not about to break radio silence on the off chance of getting an answer, but it was one more thing, one more variable, he had to consider.

Captain Karpov, the commander of the column striking north from Colonel Feyodr Yeshev's anti-tank reconnaissance regiment of the First Guards Tank Army, had been more concerned with caution than with speed, until the second message from the lost tanks was relayed to him, reporting that they were under attack. The day before, when he had led his detachment of T-80s north from the headquarters area, his primary concern was getting through the narrow stretch of uncontaminated countryside that allowed him into the clean areas where their men were trapped. It was like moving through a canyon with invisible walls and unseen precipices, and he had to tap his way along using his radiation counters like a blind man's cane. For despite the list of honors and medals that attested his bravery, Captain Karpov was by nature a cautious man. He was thankful that the second message had not come until he was nearly clear of the dead zone.

Darkness had caught them still twenty kilometers from his lost comrades' last reported position, and Karpov had ordered a halt for the night in a small deserted village in the Jura, the only one for many kilometers around. The patrol he sent out to scout the last location should be returning soon, and he was anxious to have their report. He hated being without specific orders or having to improvise. The patrol's intelligence would at least give him some basis for making a decision. He hoped it would be a decision to fight. Karpov was a good soldier and a loyal Russian. His deep doubts about the wisdom of the Soviet military planners had been sublimated into anger at the NATO Allies. He blamed them for the humiliating posture his army had been forced into by Kettle's intransigence. Usually skeptical of the lectures they received from the political officers, Karpov was willing to embrace this particular fiction, and he was eager to take out his shame and frustration on any Allied forces that crossed his path. The tales of the Allied raiders and their amazing tank did not daunt him, for he felt his dozen T-80s the equal of anything he was likely to encounter in the limbo land between the strike line and the Black Forest.

Where was that damned patrol?

Tag heard his name spoken and whirled in his bedroll, snatching his 9mm automatic from the shoulder harness on the ground beside him.

"Tag, it's Randall." And the Green Beret captain moved out of the moon-cast shadow of a beech and hunkered in front of him. Even in this light, Tag could see that the man's face was drawn and tired beneath its camouflage paint. Tag holstered his Beretta.

"Sorry," he said. "Guess I'm a little jumpy. What's up?"

"Bad news," Randall said. "We did a little snoop and poop last night back around those Ruskie tanks, just to see if we'd missed anybody or overlooked anything. Well, we've got company."

Tag knew that Randall didn't have to clear anything with him, but he was irritated just the same. Still, it brought him instantly and fully awake, all the fantods of his imagination banished. "Who?" he said. "Give it to me."

"Can't be sure," the lanky captain said. "There was just one tank, with some extra men on board who dismounted to scout the area on foot, poking into all the tanks. They may have been some more strays, but they sure acted like they knew what they were looking for. Looked well fed and well armed, too. Not like that other bunch."

"Shit," Tag said. "I think you're right, Randall. The gee-two from yesterday's satellite shots showed a column moving more or less this way from the main body of the First Guards. Did you see where they went?"

"Southwest. I should have snatched one of them, but at first we didn't know they had come in with a tank—it was a T-80, by the way. We followed them on foot, but once they were mounted up again, we couldn't get close enough, and I thought it might be better not to give ourselves away with a LAW. As it stands, they don't know for sure that we're here."

Tag offered the canteen to Randall, who took a long drink.

"Yeah," said Tag, "I guess so. I can get us a shot from the Early Bird in about an hour. Maybe it can tell us something."

"How do you do that?" Randall asked.

Tag inclined his head over his shoulder, in the direction of the No Slack Too, and said, "Brother Randall, we have more systems than a freaking aircraft carrier. Think your guys can get some rack before we have to move?"

"Where to?"

"Depending on the Early Bird pictures, I'm going to say we go on to the village. Otherwise, I'd have to let Prentice know."

"Okay by me," said Randall as he got to his feet and stretched. "Goddamn. I'da been a musician, if I knew I was going to have to sleep days." And he ambled off, melding with the night shadows.

The satellite images that Fruits Tutti conjured from the No Slack Too's superconductor bubble-chip computers and his own custom software were unmistakable: six Soviet T-80 tanks were leaving the village, moving west, away from the raiders. Not another piece of armor was visible, and the village showed no signs of life.

Tag shook his head and tutted his tongue. "Ivan is making it easy for us," he said.

"Too damn easy for me," said Ham Jefferson. "I think I smell a sucker punch."

"Maybe not, Ham," said Tag. "There's been some funny movement out of First Guards toward the Black Forest farther south. These guys might be part of that, probing the flank."

Ham snorted.

"Look, *Sergeant* Jefferson," Tag said, "we have our orders. I can change them, but there's no clear reason to do so, risk our mission and Prentice or abort the whole thing."

"You are the boss," Ham said.

Captain Karpov did not need long to make his decision. He was certain that the lost tanks had been attacked by the American tank commando who called himself Butcher Boy. Everyone knew of him. And Karpov was equally certain that Butcher Boy was still around. There had been no Allied troops in this village since the first week of the invasion, and Butcher Boy would want to have a look. Karpov also suspected that the American was, somehow, receiving satellite intelligence. He immediately ordered half of his crews into a formation on the west side of the village, and left the other six hidden in the buildings they had invested the night before, a stay-behind ambush.

An hour after dawn, he moved out at the head of the column to the west. Once in the cover of the forest, he turned them north and east, looping back on the approach to the village from the crest of the Jura.

Tag took point himself, with the Special Ops team and several of the Rangers riding in the open on the deck of the No Slack Too. The rest of the Rangers were crammed into N. Sain's Bradley, which followed Tag in the formation, with the Jagd Kommandos at flank and drag.

The morning was chill, only a degree or two shy of frost, and Tag's eyes smarted tears as he drove with his head through the hatch, winding through a series of firebreaks and old horse paths that crosshatched the crest of the mountains. The slopes were not all so gentle here as farther east, and rocky gullies sometimes cut the old paths or forced their flanks in almost to column. It took Tag longer than he had hoped to reach the firebreak that they could follow to the road they would take to the village. The firebreak itself was deeply eroded from the recent rains, and the vines and scrub at the edges of the woods on either side made getting off the track difficult once they began their descent.

Tag halted the column and put out a fire team in the woods on each flank, allowing them five minutes head start, then led N. Sain's Bradley and the three Jagd Kommando vehicles onto the firebreak.

They were wallowing through a stretch of difficult erosion gullies when Karpov's ambush hit them.

The Ranger team on the right flank tripped the ambush just as the rest of the Allied column was coming even with them. Sergeant White, the team leader, heard the electro-hydraulic hum of a T-80 turret rotating and ordered his men to prime their LAWs. But as he was fanning them out to envelope on the sound, another Soviet tank spotted the Rangers and alerted the others. Before the Rangers were in position to attack, the ambush erupted, and they were raked with machine-gun fire from the tank that had first seen them, killing two and wounding White in the hip.

Karpov had laid four of his tanks along the side of the firebreak, with two others farther down the slope on each side, their guns trained along the axis of the path. When he sprang the ambush, one of the four took out the Ranger team, and the remaining three unleashed a salvo at the raiders.

To Tag, riding with his head out of the hatch, the entire world seemed to explode around him. Two of the rounds from the T-80s struck the No Slack Too, one smashing into the troop-shield fin on the right rear of the turret, killing Randall, the Special Ops leader, one of his men, and one of the Rangers riding there. The second shot skimmed the armor on the short, sloping glacis of the XM-F4 and detonated in the trees on the other side of the firebreak. The shot from the third T-80 struck the earth two meters from the nose of the trailing Bradley, splattering it with shrapnel that whanged off the slick-skin armor like gravel off a boxcar.

"Ambush. Ambush," Tag shouted over the TacNet. "Scatter." But it was not necessary.

The harmless miss had not slowed N. Sain for an instant. When the explosion blossomed before him, the renegade reservist accelerated at once for the hole blown in the confining wall of brush by the shot that had nicked the glacis of the No Slack Too. Before the Soviet gunners could reload, he was into the trees and out of sight.

Neither did Giesla and her Kommandos need the command. While the other two cars executed lightning bootleggers' turns, she sprayed the tree line with the minigun on the nose of her gun buggy and slammed her vehicle into reverse, screaming at Horst, her loader, to find them a gap in the trees.

Tag cocked open both throttles and sent the No Slack Too lurching and bouncing out of the erosion ditches, slewing wildly back and forth across the width of the firebreak, while Ham spun the turret toward the fire and Fruits keyed the Phalanx on the afterimages on the heat-sensor sight.

"Gunner's choice," Tag said, fighting the controls with one hand and dogging down his hatch with the other.

Ham and Fruits were already at their jobs. Firing the Phalanx in a sustained sweep of the trees, Fruits threw up a hellish racket as the depleted-uranium slugs ripped tree trunks and detonated in earsplitting concussions. By luck, one round struck the main tube of a T-80 and blasted it back like a banana peel. Firing blind and through the protective screen of timber, he was not able to bring to bear the concentration of fire from the 37mm necessary to eat through the armor of a T-80, but the force of the impacts from rounds that did find their targets was enough to disrupt Karpov's next salvo.

Ham had better results. Locking his own gun onto the images from the Phalanx's heat-sensitive radar, he triggered a sabot from the 120mm that tore through the armor on the glacis of one of the ambushers. The internal explosion that rocked the Soviet tank lifted its turret from its cogs, and black-limned fire gushed from the gap, instantly incinerating the men inside.

The tank that had machine-gunned White and his team came rushing forward from its reserve position when its commander saw the tank hit by Ham's shot go up in flames. White, with the help of the other surviving Ranger, had managed to strip the LAWs from the two killed in the onslaught and drag himself into the cover of a low-limbed fir tree, where the other man was trying desperately to stop the bleeding from the fist-size crater that the 12.7mm had gouged in

White's hip. When the T-80 came forward and into White's line of sight, the young former supply sergeant said to the even younger PFC with him, "Okay, Nicky, it's hero time. Get yourself a LAW and hand me one."

The T-80 slowed to maneuver past a stand of saplings, offering itself broadside to the two Rangers at less than fifty meters. "You take the front, and I'll take the rear," White said to his man. "Let's do it."

The two Rangers fired almost simultaneously. Only in the best of circumstances could the light antitank rockets be expected to puncture the primary armor of a main battle tank, but that was not White's intention. The Rangers had trained their sights on the tracks of the T-80. The twin explosions disintegrated the track assembly and suspension on the left of the Soviet tank, and spurting hydraulic fluids washed the side of it in slow-spreading flame. The turret of the T-80 turned toward the Rangers, its barrel poking through the fire, and White took up a second LAW. Sweating with pain, shock, and adrenaline, he fumbled with the latches to release the telescoping tube.

Realizing that he was taking hits on his tanks and that Tag, as a result, had cleared the main body of the ambush, Karpov pulled his T-80 from the formation and ordered those who could to close on the two-tank blocking force farther down the slope. Only the tank with the ruined barrel could respond. Karpov rushed within twenty meters of White and the tank disabled by the LAWs.

Giesla and her Jagd Kommandos had found their way into the woods and were tacking through the timber, headed for the sounds of fighting, when she saw Karpov's tank flashing through the trees and turned toward it. Jockeying for a shot, she came into the open timber as the tank White had hit leveled its gun on the two Rangers' position. She braked, activated one of the War Clubs on the rack above the roll cage, and released it before the Soviet gunner could get off a shot. The needle-nosed missile screamed from its mount and parted the armor on the T-80 just above its track skirt, penetrating the engine housing and exploding in a rivet-popping eruption of steel and expanding gases that tore through the crew compartment and blew out the rear grille. The cars with Betcher and Jan in the drivers' seats roared up from behind, and she ordered them to tend to the Rangers, then sped away herself in pursuit of Karpov and the other T-80.

Tag was driving hell-for-leather straight into the awaiting guns of the two Soviets controlling the lower stretch of the firebreak, when he saw N. Sain's Bradley break into view up ahead, racing up-slope toward him. An image of an L-shaped ambush leapt to Tag's mind.

"Bumps," he called to his crew, and threw the No Slack Too into a hard left turn across a series of washes, angling for what he hoped was a gap in the timber behind the wall of vines and saplings. It saved their lives. A shot from one of the awaiting T-80s caromed off the wedge-shaped edge of the XM-F4 at a sharp angle, knocking the No Slack Too off its course but causing no serious damage. Tag hit the trees at open throttle, carrying yards of vines across the nose of his tank and locking tracks madly to bend around the maze of trunks that blocked him from the action.

When he saw Tag react, N. Sain, his Bradley now emptied of Rangers, who were moving on line through the forest, steered his APC back into the woods as well and nearly collided with one of the T-80s parked there. He triggered his phalanx system and never veered from his course, boring into the Soviet armor with a stream from the 37mm gun the way a fire hose cuts through mud. As the inside layers of the T-80's steel-and-glass composite armor gave way, its crew was swarmed by white-hot fragments, followed by lethal bursts of depleted-uranium cores.

Karpov and his trailing tank crashed upon the scene at the moment N. Sain broke off his attack and sheared away from his target, the wailing turbines of the Bradley carrying it past the approaching Russian before Karpov could react.

Realizing that he was losing all his advantage, as well as half of his tanks, Karpov ordered his unit to break contact and follow him. But before the tank on the other side of the firebreak could respond, Giesla had the tank with the shattered barrel in her sights, and a pair of armor-piercing rounds from her 106mm recoilless rifle tubes slammed into it from the rear. The massive Soviet MBT shuddered once before its fuel tanks exploded and ripped a gaping hole through the rear deck, spreading burning fuel like napalm.

Karpov reversed his course and in the cover of the flames shot through the woods and across the firebreak, screaming over his radio for the lone surviving T-80 to follow him east. The other tank commander was only too happy to oblige. He jammed his vehicle into a pivoting turn on one track and gave it full throttle. Driving recklessly, ricocheting off trees and crashing through dips in the forest floor, the fleeing tankers did not see the camouflaged forms of the Rangers dispersed in the woods. Of the three LAWs fired by the Rangers, two hit armor plate, causing only minor damage, but the third found enough of the rear grille to send a spume of dark smoke uncoiling from the T-80's exhaust. The tank coughed and slowed but somehow kept going, and soon was out of sight among the trees.

Cursing the thicket he had charged into, Tag worked his steering yoke and throttles and extricated the No Slack Too from the vines, brush, and small timber just in time to see the two Soviets escape, but not soon enough to get back in the fight. He keyed the TacNet and said, "All elements, this is Butcher Boy. Rally on me, in the open."

He broke back through onto the firebreak, and within minutes the vehicles had all found him and the Rangers were beginning to come in on foot.

The gathering was not a happy one for Tag. It took a while to account for everyone, but the final total showed Captain Randall and one other of the Green Berets killed, along with three Rangers, in addition to a half dozen wounded, including White, whose hip had stiffened and begun to hurt so badly that he had to be carried. Even so, they had destroyed four Soviet main battle tanks and had all of their own vehicles intact.

Gaylord Krager said, "That's right, Max, and one of those that got away was limping bad. He'd be easy pickin's."

Tag thought fast. "Giesla," he said, "you can carry a third man in each of your cars, can't you?"

"If they can sit, yes," she said.

"Okay, here's what I want you to do: get Sergeant White and the other two who need serious attention and put them in with you. Trail those other two tanks for a way and try to pick them off. If you can't do that easily, go ahead and get our wounded back to base camp. Make contact with Prentice, if you can, then all of you meet us at the village."

Giesla nodded. "We will be there," she said.

Karpov was a shattered man, shattered and terrified. After witnessing the No Slack Too absorb direct hits from his tanks and only intensify its counterassault, he was shocked and rattled. But as the other elements of the raider command struck back, and his armor began dropping like flies, he was pushed into a panic. Only the discipline of his training kept him from full flight and abandoning his crippled comrade. He had no stomach for doubling back and risking another encounter with Butcher Boy in order to reach the rest of his unit waiting in the village. Right now, the wasteland of the nuclear strike zone looked like an oasis to him. He ordered the damaged tank to move ahead of him, on a direct course for the dead zone.

Giesla and the Jagd Kommandos had to move slowly, because of their wounded passengers, but it was almost fast enough for them to overtake the two T-80s. She kept up the chase for nearly a half hour, until it was clear where they were headed. She was disgruntled over being unable to deliver a final blow against the ambushers but satisfied that they were out of the fight altogether.

She ordered the Jagd Kommandos to button up their NBC defenses and steered them all toward their alternative bolt hole, a path across the strike zone that showed pale yellow on the radiation overlays. The woods were irradiated and had lost their foliage, although they were still standing here, and she hoped the gun buggies would not pick up too much residual contamination. She was already anxious to be back with Tag and did not want to linger at base camp while

the technicians decontaminated them. Sgt. White was
also in much discomfort, despite the morphine he had
been given, so Giesla pushed her people forward. Once
out of the strike zone, they took again to the old trails
and logging roads and made good time back to the
redoubt in the mineworks.

As Giesla and the Jagd Kommandos were passing
through the zone, Prentice was reentering it farther
north, carrying resupplies of fuel and ammunition in
the back of his empty Bradley. He felt an urgency that
he could not account for. Perhaps it had to do with
the radio silence they were maintaining, and perhaps
with the grimness in Barlow's voice when the black
colonel told him that the raiders' mission now included search-and-destroy operations against all targets
of opportunity. Most of all, however, Prentice had
the feeling that Tag's unit was not as anonymous
as it had once been. The wild dash that Tag had
made through the heart of the First Guards' positions
four weeks before had let Ivan see the XM-F4 up
close and personal. Prentice was not superstitious,
didn't believe in premonitions or bad vibes, as N.
Sain would say, but he did have a bad feeling about
the way things were developing. Sixty days ago he
had been a green-as-grass supply officer, edgy about
everything and uncertain of his own mettle. Now he
was as hardened a veteran as any in Europe. He
had proved himself a good soldier and was easy in
that confidence. That made his unease all the more
profound to him. He wished to hell that Tag would
quit being so damned optimistic. A good soldier, like
a good baseball manager, knows that it ain't over till
it's over.

Deep in the middle of the dead zone, he began

picking up a smattering of garbled radio traffic that he could tell was from the Jagd Kommandos. That could mean only one of two things. Either some of the Kommandos had crossed back over the line or something had happened to cause them to break silence. In either case, there was something going on that was not in the plans when he left early that morning to deliver the prisoners back to base.

Prentice scanned his maps and the now-familiar landscape of the strike zone. Adrenaline worked on him, clarifying his memory of the trip in, bringing back each detail of their route with perfect clarity. He urged the young Ranger at the controls of the Bradley to speed up, his voice taking an edge of impatience as he issued the commands. Two of the things he had learned about being a good soldier were trust and loyalty. He had learned to trust his men, and that inspired confidence in them, and he had developed a powerful loyalty to Tag, the man who had taught him that lesson. Prentice imagined horrible things he would do to Ivan if Tag came to harm, and he was shocked by the ferocity of his own thoughts. He had never before imagined pulling a man's face from his skull.

4

Once Giesla had been dispatched with the badly wounded, and the dead had been buried, the remaining Rangers crowded aboard N. Sain's Bradley, and Tag moved them and the No Slack Too down the firebreak.

After less than a kilometer, the slope flattened, and a narrow road paved in macadam intersected the firebreak. Farther down the mountain, Tag could see in glimpses through the trees the wink of bright water, the headwaters of the romantic Danube that tumbled through mountain gorges and into the turbines of a hydroelectric generating plant, abandoned by its operators in the first days of the war. The morning had warmed the southern face of the Jura to the temperature of high autumn, and the dry air was bracing. Tag opened his hatch and let the wind run across his face for about five kilometers down the paved road, then he halted in the shade of trees in a small park by the side of the road overlooking the valley of the Danube.

The Rangers piled out of the Bradley, grateful for the break from its cramped troop compartment, and dispersed in a loose perimeter to eat. Tag called N. Sain, Krager, and the two squad leaders, Dunn and Villalobos, to a meeting at his tank.

"I've been scoping out the road," he said, "and it doesn't look to me like there's been any traffic coming this way, except for the boys from the ambush. We're about three klicks from our objective right now, and there's no place between here and there where Ivan could hit us. So, when we move out, it's going to be fast."

"So," Krager said, "what's the drill when we hit the vil, Max?"

"That's the rub, Gaylord," said Tag. "The damned burg is practically hanging on the side of the mountain. There's a ridge around it to the north, but most of the town is built on these transverse ridges, except for a few blocks right in the center." He paused and called to Fruits Tutti inside the No Slack Too. "Hey, Fruits, print me out four or five details of the village, on topo grids."

"Yeah, yeah," Fruits whined from inside the turret. "I'll do dat *too*."

"Okay," Tag continued, "here's what I think. The satellite gee-two that we first got on these bad guys showed us twelve tanks. We know what happened to six of them, but the question is: what about the other half dozen? My hunch is that they're still in the village."

"What makes you think that?" Krager asked.

"Just a hunch, Gaylord. We know there were twelve, and we don't have anything to tell us that they split up, turned back, or anything."

Krager sucked his cheeks. "Why, Max?" he asked. "Why would they stay behind?"

"Being held in reserve, left there to hold a base camp, maybe they are even gone, sneaked out on patrol when our satellite window was shut. I don't know. But we're going to go in strong."

N. Sain shifted from foot to foot. "O Avatar of Ambush," he intoned. "Mighty Samson was blinded by his own strength. Could we not let our eyes guide us?"

Villalobos said to Dunn, "What the hell is he talking about?"

"I think he means for us to scout the vil on foot first," Dunn replied. "Ain't that right, Captain?"

"No way," said Tag. "If we do that, and if Ivan decides to run, there's no way we could get into position in time to stop him, not with just the No Slack Too and one Bradley to cover both ends of town."

"Hey, Captain Max," Fruits called from the turret hatch, "here's youse guys' maps." He climbed down onto the fender of the No Slack Too and gave the printouts to Tag.

"Thanks, Fruits," Tag said, taking the maps and handing them to N. Sain, Krager, Dunn, and Villalobos. "Here's what I want to do," Tag told them. "N. Sain, you take Gaylord and the Rangers up around this flat-topped ridge to the north. When you get to the other side of town, lay in an ambush. Put the Bradley here, at the corner, to anchor it. Gaylord, you deploy your men along here, to cover the road. It's the only way any T-80s could get out. I'm taking the No Slack

Too into the village. If there are any bogeys inside, we may flush 'em right over you. Otherwise, don't shoot us when we come out."

"Max," said Krager, "with all due respect, I don't like this. Prentice and the jay-kays will be back in a few hours. Don't you think we could wait on them?"

Tag dismissed the suggestion with a wave of his hand. "No point, Gaylord," he said. "Assuming that I'm right and there are some bogeys still here, we can handle 'em. I want to get this little piece of work out of the way, because the way things are happening right now, SACEUR may need us for something else right away."

"Yes, sir," Krager said. "Let's do it, then."

While he gave N. Sain and Krager time to maneuver into position, Tag indulged himself in some serious self-examination. Krager was an old hooking bull, and he was apt to question a plan just for the sake of testing it. N. Sain was another matter, however, and his reluctance caused Tag to look at what he was doing in a different light. Maybe the rock 'n' roll warrior was finally getting some savvy and was, for a change, trying to put a meaningful oar in the water, because Tag had no question of the man's bravery. But it was unlike N. Sain to question anything that would lead him into combat. Still, Tag could not deny that the man had an idiot savant's knack for warfare, and if his reluctance about Tag's plan was real, it might mean something.

Tag watched the hyper-Bradley disappear into the timber as it quartered up the slope, and he thought about his own feelings these past weeks. Wheels's death and his own wound had not passed without impact, one even greater than his conscious realization of the limitations of the XM-F4. Like every soldier, Tag held his own mortality as an abstraction. Death was always near, but it was something that happened to others. This was, he knew, a necessary fiction, one that had sustained men through wars and battles as long as there had been wars and battles. But it had come awfully close to him this time. Perhaps it was that very nearness that had led him to denying even the possibility of his own death, a denial that he reinforced with unnecessary risks and unfounded optimism. Perhaps N. Sain had been right . . .

Ham Jefferson snapped Tag out of his self-doubts. "Hey, boss," the gunner said over the intercom, "how do we dress for town?"

"Sabot," Tag said. "Fruits, you stand by on the Phalanx. I'll command the War Clubs."

Tag spun the turbines to life and set them to whisper mode before he engaged the gears and accelerated out of the park and onto the macadam. In two minutes they were in sight of the village, and Tag could see the maze of steep, winding streets that crawled through its hills and hollows, following the contours of the land without regard for surveyors' lines or the convenience of motor traffic. It was a town of necessity, first settled by heretic Protestants to escape both the dictates of state faith and the Catholic Inquisition. The road the No Slack Too was traveling lost itself in that labyrinth, only to emerge again on the other side, where N. Sain and the Rangers should now be waiting. Tag stopped long enough to scan once with his audio-directional sensor, but the stout rock and timbers of the houses and buildings muffled any sound there might have been. He wiped his palms once on his thighs and said, "Stand to. We're going in."

He kicked open the throttles, flew down the short grade on the approach to town, and felt the vibration

inside the XM-F4 change as the blacktop gave over
to the cobblestones of the streets.

The Soviet lieutenant left in command of the stay-
behind ambush in the village got word of Tag's
approach over a field telephone from one of his
crews stationed at the edge of town, in a second-story
garage that commanded a view of the road. But rather
than ordering the tank to fire on the No Slack Too, the
lieutenant, suspecting that there were more to follow,
let Tag pass. Only after some minutes did he order
the T-80 out of the garage and have it move in on the
Americans from the rear.

The No Slack Too shot past the buildings on the
outskirts of the village with all of its detection systems engaged—radar, audio link, heat sensors, and
NBC counters—each of them feeding data through
Tag's main terminal display, which itself offered him
an image of such clarity that it was like looking
through a window on the world. Tag could view
the information from his systems in a series of small
readout boxes that ran along one edge of the screen,
and he was glad to have their capabilities, for he knew
his strategy was neither subtle nor much admired by
most tankers. Relying on the sensors and the No Slack
Too's first-hit survivability, he was making himself
the bait in his own trap, hoping that any lurking
Soviets would give themselves away with a shot that
he could then counter. He had not bothered to discuss
this plan with his crew or comrades.

The street on which he had entered the town turned
sharply uphill after less than two blocks—or what
amounted to two blocks, for there were no cross
streets—broke over the top of a ridge, and descended

steeply into a street down a winding hollow lined by beetling houses. To his left, another street looped back toward the top of the ridge before rejoining the one through the hollow. It reminded Tag of a small town called Eureka Springs in the Arkansas Ozarks, where he had once stayed while on a trout-fishing trip with a friend from Fort Hood. None of the streets ran straight; there were no right-angle intersections; and most of the hillside houses could be entered from any of their floors. In Eureka Springs, Tag had once driven for a half hour, trying to get to a restaurant he could see across a ravine, only to arrive each time back at the place where he had started. But that had been in a rented Jeep, not in an XM-F4 tank with LandNav computers and satellite maps.

Tag's first objective was the few square blocks of relatively flat land near the center of town, where there was a church, a town hall, and some businesses clustered around a tiny square, with its fountain of spring water burbling in the middle. His route took him past a second of the T-80s parked in the lobby of a small hostel. On orders from the lieutenant, it too let him pass, followed shortly by the Soviet crew who had first seen the No Slack Too enter the town.

Tag could see that the town had not been shelled, and so a building with a wall knocked out did not escape his attention, but he still could suspect that the damage had been done by previous Soviet patrols, perhaps even by the contingent of T-80s they had defeated in the ambush on the firebreak. He was all eyes and ears now, however, as each block that they penetrated into the village roused new suspicions and concerns in him.

The final approach he was taking to the town square was up a winding street with no intersections. Near

the top of it, he suddenly spun the No Slack Too
around and said to his crew, "Something doesn't smell
right here."

"Hey, boss," Ham Jefferson said, "the hair on my
neck's been crawlin' for ten minutes, like they's somebody lookin' at me."

"Well, we're gonna have a look back, Ham. Shoot
anything that moves."

Tag spun the XM-F4's treads on the slick cobbles,
hauling the thirty tons of fighting machine through the
descending curves of the street like a slalom skier.
Coming out of the third, he saw the trailing T-80 just
starting up the grade.

"Shoot," he said, but the order was lost in the roar
and recoil from the No Slack Too's 120mm gun, as
an integral-propellant sabot screamed from the tube.
The penetrator core of the projectile struck the Soviet
turret directly above the gun mantle, splitting the
thick armor like a melon rind. The explosion in the
T-80's ammunition magazine blew away every piece
of bolt-ons—hatches, grilles, and track carriage—as
blades of flame slashed through the openings. The
tank seemed to collapse on its suspension and was at
once engulfed in smoke, entirely blocking the street.

Tag never paused. He locked one tread and turned
the No Slack Too back uphill, accelerating as he
did.

"Okay," he said over the intercom, "curtain's up,
and we're on. Watch for your cues."

The XM-F4 barreled back up the hill and sprang
over the lip into the square like a pouncing panther.
Tag feinted left, then on some vague instinct juked
hard to the right and started counterclockwise around
the small park in the center of the square. He knew
he had been fired on when the facade of a building

behind him disintegrated in a shower of smoke, dust, and rock. A heat blip on his liquid-crystal display marked the target in a narrow alley on the far side of the square. The angle was too great for Ham to have a clear shot at the body of the T-80, and his counterfire struck a wall of one of the buildings beside the alley, bringing down two stories of rock and timber on top of the Soviet tank.

Tag skidded the No Slack Too in a turn toward a street roughly parallel to the alley. The steel tracks gnawed the tops off cobbles as the tank scratched for traction. Fishtailing like a drag strip hot rod, Tag flattened two lampposts and a bicycle rack before he squared up on the street and shot forward to the howl of spinning turbines and slashing tracks.

A half-dozen doors off the square, the street split in a Y, and Tag took the right-hand fork, back up the grade, which he knew would, after a series of zigzag turns, bring him back on the square again from above. Near the highest point on the jagged circuit, his sensors flashed, and a T-80 hidden in a garage dug into the mountainside wheeled out onto the street behind him. Just ahead of him a house beetled far out from the face of the mountain, supported above the street on log stilts the size of telephone poles. Tag veered beneath it, taking out the stilts like ten-pins, barely clearing the avalanche of masonry that came down, blocking the narrow street.

Tag's eyes were bright as diamonds, and his grin twice as hard. He was rapt in the action now, fighting with a furious clarity that transcended thought, and Fruits and Ham were likewise infected with his mania-cal intensity, achieving that oneness of thought and action that had made them the best crew ever to ride in armor. No one needed to speak; no orders were necessary. Each of them acted as one, and that one was the paradigm of tank warfare, the embodiment of Ross Kettle's vision that had brought the XM-F4 to reality and brought them to be the decisive factor in the fate of the Allied counterattack.

Tag reentered the square from the north and at once saw the T-80 that had been buried beneath the rubble trying to dislodge itself from the alley.

"Fruits," he said, "Phalanx target."

"Roger dodger," Fruits replied, tripping the electronic trigger on the Gatling-barreled 37mm. The exploding cores of depleted uranium from the gun threw up a shroud of smoke and dust from the debris that was the death pall for the Communist tankers, as the slugs bored through their armor and filled the crew compartment with shards of swarming death. The driver of the T-80 fell dead at his sticks, jamming open his throttle, and the motor of the steel coffin that had been a main battle tank revved out of control, until its bearings let go in a sick-sounding convulsion of machinery consuming itself, and the tank came to a smoking halt against a standing wall.

Tag skittered the No Slack Too around the square again and onto the same street he had taken just minutes before. At the Y, he shot into the left-hand fork, and called to Ham, "Turret rear."

The gunner spun the turret as Tag braked them to a stop. The tank that Tag had blocked by the house he brought down came tearing back down the street toward the square. When it passed the Y, exposing its rear to Ham's sights, the 120mm bucked back in its dampers. The round did not travel far enough for the sabot to separate from the penetrator before it struck the T-80 turret from behind, lifting it from the body of the tank with a concussion that the men inside the No Slack Too could feel. The turret flew forward over the glacis and came to rest in the center of the square, water from the fountain hissing on the hot armor, while the body of the tank sat like a decapitated animal, smoke coiling from its wound.

Tag rapidly reviewed the situation. The main approach from the east was blocked, as was the loop road connecting the square with the ridge to the north, and if Ivan was smart, there would be no more action around the square itself. More likely, the remaining Soviets—and Tag was certain now that there were more—would stay in their ambush sites and wait for him, or they would attempt to corner him. Well, he thought, let's give them something to do.

He pulled the No Slack Too next to one of the buildings that had an ornamental iron fire escape hanging off its side and said to his crew, "Fruits, get down here and take the yoke. Ham, be on your toes. I'm going naked."

He took his binoculars from their cubby hole, unbuckled himself, and shinnied up into the turret as Fruits climbed down, then went out the turret hatch and hauled himself onto the adjacent fire escape. His boot rang on the iron treads as he hurried to the top, where a narrow catwalk ran between the cornice and the building's mansard roof.

Tag low-crawled along the catwalk, his profile broken by a low, spiked railing, until he reached the corner. From there, he could see most of the village to the north, south, and west. He lay still for several minutes, listening and looking with his naked eye, before he raised the binoculars and began to scan the streets and roofs. The village was still as death, without so much as a cat to be seen. The primary route through town, an extension of the street below, dipped down the slope before it climbed back to rejoin the narrow blacktop to the west. That had to be it, he decided. Surely Ivan would not neglect to cover the obvious. There were other, less direct routes he could take out of town, but his purpose was to fight not hide. Giving the village a last once-over, he spotted an anomaly, a new building under construction, its street-side facade complete and the rest still just framework. Tag studied it for a minute before he wriggled around and crawled back to the fire escape and down to the No Slack Too.

"Here's the drill, gentlemen," he said to Fruits and Ham. "We're going to travel the main route out of town to the west. If we don't make any contact, we'll sweep the whole vil again with the Rangers and N. Sain. But don't count on us getting lucky. I don't think we're through with Ivan here yet."

He gave a quick glance at his systems and moved the XM-F4 forward at a fast walk. After a series of short, sharp bends, the street swept down the mountain in a long grade, making a hairpin turn at the bottom for its ascent to the highway. Several smaller streets forked off the main drag, some dead ends, some connecting with other meandering avenues, and others circling back on themselves. Any one of them could hold an ambush.

Tag eased the No Slack Too down the grade in low gear, the turbines muted to a whisper, adrenaline fluttering in his throat.

"Fruits," he said, "keep the Phalanx trained rear and cover our six."

Tag armed the War Club missiles.

A shadow moved in the mouth of a side street near the bottom of the grade, and simultaneously the 360-degree radar detected motion to the rear. Tag slapped the transmission into high range and booted open the throttles, shouting over the intercom, "Keep their heads down, Fruits."

The trip-hammer recoil of the 37mm shuddered through the No Slack Too as Fruits filled the space between the buildings behind them with slugs. Tag marked the movement ahead of them on his screen and ordered Ham to shoot. The gunner released the sabot in his tube, shattering the wall of an apartment flat. Tag slung the XM-F4 through the hairpin, blinded by the dust and smoke from Ham's shot, and came out of it as a third T-80 emerged at the top of the hill ahead of him. He loosed one of the War Clubs from its clam-shell faring on the side of the turret, but he fired too fast, before he had a solid lock, and the needle-nosed missile plowed into the cobbled street in front of the descending Soviet tank, throwing up another screen of debris. Immediately he hit the smoke button, releasing a thick billow of white from the rear of the No Slack Too, and snapped the yoke to the right, heading into one of the narrow looping streets.

Suddenly the American tank had vanished. The Soviet lieutenant coming down the street charged into the smoke, braced for a collision that never came, and emerged from it into the hairpin bend, nearly hitting his comrade closing from the other direction. The third tank, dusted with powdered brick and mortar, wheeled out onto the street to protect its leader's rear, then all three stopped in confusion.

The lieutenant was growing panicky. He shouted over his radio, screaming at the other tank commanders to advance into the streets on the high side. As the two bulky T-80s at the bottom of the turn

maneuvered themselves around, and the one covering the ascending slope disappeared back into the
thinning smoke screen, the front of an unfinished
building exploded out into the street, spouting tongues
of flame.

Tag had calculated right. The ambush he himself
would have laid came down as he expected. Under
the cover of fire and smoke, he had turned the No
Slack Too up the circling street above the hairpin and
came in from the rear of the half-finished structure he
had seen earlier. Turning as wide as possible for a run
at the wood-framed skeleton, Tag gave the No Slack
Too full throttle, saying to his crew, "Shoot 'em when
you see 'em."

The two-by-six framing splintered like dry straw
when the XM-F4 hit it but remained standing until
the tank struck the facade of false half-timbering,
blasting through it in a shower of rubble. The two
T-80s were no more than twenty meters from the
No Slack Too when Tag released another War Club
from the racks and Ham triggered the 120mm. All
at once, the building collapsed like a house of cards;
the War Club pierced one T-80 through the glacis;
and Ham's shot gouged a puckered, ragged hole in
the side of the second. The first Soviet tank bucked
forward as though it had hit a wall, and the other
stopped in its tracks. Then, both were rocked by
explosions inside them that blasted back through the
entry holes, scorching the nose and one side of the
No Slack Too.

With the incinerating T-80s obscuring his heat sensors, it took Tag a moment to check off on his target
acquisition systems and locate the third T-80 on his
radar, fleeing up the hill.

"Fruits, target," he called out, and Fruits Tutti raked the dissipating smoke with the Phalanx. The curve of the street was just enough to prevent him from getting a clean shot, and the rounds that did find the tank were not enough to chew through the armor.

"Dammit," Tag swore as the blip disappeared from his screen. "Hang on, cowboys."

There was not enough room on either side of the tank Ham had hit for the No Slack Too to pass between it and the buildings facing the street, and the wreckage of the unfinished building that Tag had crashed through blocked that path as well. He rammed the rear quarter of the T-80 at half throttle, backed off, and did it again and again until he could scrape by, taking out the glass and doors of the storefront on his left.

He flew through the last wisps of the smoke screen he had laid down and screamed up the street, gaining speed to the top of the hill, then slowed for a series of turns that brought him onto a short, straight stretch leading to the highway out of town. When he came at last to the open road, all there was to see was a smoldering pile of junk in the middle of it.

The T-80—or what remained of it—was in more parts than anyone would want to count. Its treads were scattered like strings of snapped beads; the turret had been blown away, hanging precariously to one side by its cog ring; pieces of grille and hatches lay scattered for thirty meters around; and the body had been riddled by dozens of holes.

Tag braked to a halt and threw back his hatch. "Take a look at this, guys," he said over the intercom.

Ham and then Fruits came out of the turret hatch and stared at the smoking wreckage.

"Christ on a creepin' crutch," Fruits said.

Ham gave a sharp whistle and said, "Wasn't no N. Sain did all that, bossman."

Out of the rocks and trees on the low side of the road, Rangers began to appear, several holding expended LAWs, and from the ridge above Tag heard the sound of several engines revving up. A smile crossed his face.

"*Exactamente*, Mr. Jefferson," he said. "Looks like our good luck caught up with Ivan."

He watched the ridge as three Jagd Kommando gun buggies picked their way down the side, and two hyper-Bradleys bounced along behind them.

Ham slid off the front of the turret and squatted on the narrow forward deck beside Tag's hatch. "I imagine that just because it worked, you're gonna tell me you were right all the time—ain't you, boss?"

Tag flushed, stopped himself from speaking for a moment, then laughed and looked up at Ham sheepishly. "Hell," he said, "it *did* work, Hambone. But you're probably right: we were more lucky than good this time."

"Well," the black gunner said, "I hope to hell you got it out of your system. This shit is enough to make me join the infantry. No kidding, you doin' all right now?"

"Yeah, Ham. And thanks. I'll run it all down for you sometime, but I've got my head back on straight."

"Save your war stories for your grandkids," Ham said, slapping Tag on the shoulder. "I just want to live long enough to have some."

Giesla was in the first commando car to make it to the road, and she brought it to a screeching stop just inches from the No Slack Too. The gull-wing door on the crew cowl flew open and she sprang out, spitting mad.

"You goddamn Tag cowboy, you," she snapped, so angry that her English began to break down. "You are as bad as I first thought you were—no, worse. I thought you had no discipline, but now I think you have no sense. You think you are some sort of *Übermensch*, a buccaneer in your big bad tank?" She paused for breath, and Tag quickly cut in:

"Wait. Ham Jefferson has already done it for you. He's already boarded my ass and made me walk the plank. You're both right. Mea culpa. I screwed up. Are you happy now?"

Giesla glared at him and fumed, clenching and unclenching her fists until she was calm enough to speak.

"No," she said, lowering her voice, "except that you are alive. Come on. Chuck and I both have news for you from Barlow."

5

Colonel Yeshev was furious. Even before news of the destruction of the tanks in the village reached him, he had received a message from the survivors of the original ambush, telling him that Butcher Boy was again in the area and again wreaking havoc within the so-called neutral zone, the zone that Yeshev had been ordered to secure in preparation for a push toward the Black Forest by the First Guards Army.

The humiliation of Tag's earlier dash through the heart of the army's formations had been offset by the damage done to the No Slack Too by Yeshev's ambush of T-80Bs, the one that had kept Tag out of action for nearly a month. But while the negotiations on the fate of the First Guards had dragged on, its commanding general had become impatient, and some small things indicated to Yeshev that things in

Moscow were increasingly uncertain, political things that worried him far more than the precarious situation of the First Guards in southern Germany.

Major Viktor, Yeshev's intelligence officer and suspected KGB operative, had appeared increasingly nervous, prickly on points of party dogma, and critical of Yeshev's reservations about the ability of the general staff to rescue the First Guards. Several of the regimental political officers had been removed or replaced, and the planned push toward the Black Forest itself, which had already been dismissed once, told Yeshev that the Kremlin was willing to risk a desperate gamble. The military wisdom of the advance was nil. Therefore, its only possible rationale was political. Yeshev knew enough of the current situation in the world to know that the cease-fire was hurting no one and that the First Guards were no more or less than a political pawn in global-power negotiations. The only political advantage that the Kremlin might gain would be an internal one, rallying support for the brave heroes of the Soviet Union and deflecting opposition to Moscow's disgraced policies and strategies.

Still, Yeshev was a professional soldier, and his pride would not allow him to balk at orders so long as he saw some practical benefit that might be derived from them, even if it meant his own death or the decimation of his command. If the First Guards were to have any hope of extricating themselves from the trap that their own nuclear assault had left them in, he would have to neutralize Butcher Boy and give his army freedom to move around and through the line of nuclear contamination. The push to the Black Forest could never succeed. Their only hope lay in withdrawing to the east, smashing through the thin Allied lines, and regrouping beyond the Czechoslovakian border. But between the American satellites and that damned black tank that kept popping up like a bad kopeck, all his efforts to secure their routes had been scotched.

Throughout the day, Yeshev paced the floor of his operation bunker, while reports came in of the destruction of his tanks in the village. Captain Karpov, the commander of the detachment, who had been forced along with one other crippled T-80 into the fringes of the nuclear zone, was at last limping back toward the headquarters, and Yeshev spent much of his time fuming silently at the captain. Yeshev's bespectacled operations officer, the professional Major Minski, was the only other officer in the bunker, and he had had the good sense not to bother the colonel with superfluous details, but had spent his time thumbing through his encyclopedic memory of past situations, in the hope of finding one appropriate to the problem Yeshev now faced.

Major Viktor came into the bunker in the early afternoon, bearing the news that the Bradleys accompanying Butcher Boy were something new, able to absorb hits from a 73mm without effect, and suggesting that greater concentrations of heavy armor might be called for.

Yeshev nearly exploded.

"Nikolai," he said with barely contained exasperation, "what do you think we have been trying to do? Of course the American APCs are new. Do you think I have not been listening to the reports? How many of our tanks does your intelligence say we have already lost to this Butcher Boy, eh?"

"Many," Viktor replied.

Yeshev snorted. "Yes. Many. And we will lose

many more, unless we can devise something better than what we have already tried." He turned to Minski. "Do you have any ideas, Professor?"

Minski looked thoughtful, clasped his hands behind his back, and paced slowly in front of the situation map on the wall.

"I think," he said, "that this is without precedent. Our greatest success against the American has come when we were able to get him deep within our area of operation and ambush him. So far, it appears that he can expect no tactical support, that he is operating outside the protocols of the cease-fire, and that SACEUR will not wholly compromise the political accords to save a single commando unit. What we do not know with certainty is the kind and degree of intelligence support available. I think that before we can devise a successful strategy that we must determine this through a series of orchestrated probes that will test the American. Once we see how he reacts, we should be able to lure him into a vulnerable position and take advantage of it."

The reluctance of his operations officer to think originally often frustrated Yeshev, although he did respect the professor's knowledge and thoroughness. This time, however, he saw the wisdom of Minski's train of thought.

"And perhaps," Yeshev said, "we could arrange some disinformation to help mask the nature of our maneuvers, something to make Butcher Boy think it is not him we are after at all."

Minski nodded in agreement. "Yes, that and a movement large enough not to be mistaken for a mere patrol or foray, but something that appeared to be part of the larger advance, for I feel certain that the NATO Allies have guessed that we are poised to exercise the Black Forest option."

"But that would require at least a battalion," Viktor protested, "and we have less than two battalions at full strength in the entire regiment, Comrade Colonel."

"I believe," said Yeshev slyly, "that it was your suggestion to concentrate our efforts, was it not, Nikolai?"

Viktor stammered and fell silent.

Yeshev turned back to Major Minski. "You are right, Professor. If we can do this without exposing ourselves unnecessarily, we may get Butcher Boy to overextend himself."

Tag whistled softly between his teeth and ducked his chin beneath one shoulder, as though slipping under a punch.

"Let me get this straight," he said to Giesla. "Barlow wants us to stay out in the cold?"

"That's about it, Max," Prentice replied. "He wants us in place for something more than recon, but he was real sketchy about what that 'something more' would be. I mean, he specifically said 'search-and-destroy targets of opportunity,' all right, but you could tell there was more to it than that. Meanwhile, he wants us to take up a base position and try to make do with the resupply I brought in."

"Did you get anything else out of him, Gies?" Tag said.

Giesla shrugged. "Not a lot," she said. "My feeling is that it all has to do with the political situation. There are still many indications that the First Guards are poised for a move on the Black Forest, but there are also indications that this is not on clear orders from Moscow. The entire Black Forest offensive—or the appearance of it—may be only a gambit. I ask myself:

Why would the Soviets want to put themselves farther
behind our lines? I know that SACEUR is trying to
goad them, make them desperate, with a no-retreat,
no-surrender option, but an assault to the west and
north would be a disaster."

Tag sucked his cheek and thought for a moment.
"Okay," he said. "Orders is orders, but we'll take our
time finding a spot to make camp. Let's move every-
body up to the top of the ridge until tomorrow morning. If we've got to make do for a while, I'm going
to let our eyes in the sky do most of the searching."

Yeshev knew—as Tag did not—that the NATO
Allies had already won the war in space, knocking
out nearly all of the Soviet spy and communication satellites, but not without suffering significant
losses of American orbiters as well. Yeshev knew that
Butcher Boy was receiving satellite intelligence, but
he did not know what that included, whether it was
only visual information, or whether the radar/infrared
signals were getting through also. But he was ready
to find out.

Yeshev turned to his operations officer and said,
"Professor, here is the plan. Mobilize First Battalion
immediately and move it out toward Butcher Boy's
last-known position. After dark, bring them back and
have Second Battalion depart due north. Halt them at
least two hours before dawn and have them go into
total concealment—all engines off, full camouflage,
and absolutely no movement."

Minski's long face brightened. *Da,* Comrade Colonel, I see. I see. At once."

Once their perimeter was set, Tag had the ammunition, food, and fuel in Prentice's Bradley distributed

to his unit, then sat down with Ham and Fruits to bring them up to speed on their assignments.

"Fruits," he said, "I want you to set up our whole array of satellite receivers. One of us will be on the screens around the clock. I want every scrap of info we can get on Ivan's movements—what, where, when, how many—the whole ball of wax. Got that?"

"Yeah, I got it," Fruits said, "but I don't get it either. I mean, Captain Max, we ain't got no night vision worth a shit, 'specially' not on anything movin' within six or eight klicks of dem hot spots."

"Fruit Loops is hip, boss," Ham Jefferson said. "We just playin' with ourselves, trying to catch Ivan in the dark. Course, unless Ivan be real stupid."

"Maybe he is, and maybe not," Tag said, "but we're damn sure not gonna be. Sometime in the next thirty-six to forty-eight hours, we're going to have to go to ground, and I don't want any surprises. We've got zip for backup, sweethearts, so we play the percentages."

"So," Ham asked, resignation thick in his voice, "how long *do* we get to turn in the wind?"

Tag flashed him a big grin.

"How long we been already, Hambone?" he said.

"Jeez," Fruits muttered, "I fuggin' hate it when he talks like that."

"We the mushroom men, Tutti Fruity," Ham said. "Fed on horse shit and kept in the dark."

"Meanwhile," Tag continued, "Ham, I want you to pull preventive maintenance on the No Slack Too and then get me a complete report from Krager on the Rangers' combat status—weapons, rations, medical supplies, all that."

Tag left his two crewmen to their whining and bitching and went to find Prentice and Giesla.

The sweet reek of methanol fuel guided Tag across the wooded ridge to Prentice's Bradley, where the Jagd Kommandos were gassing up their gun buggies from the drums in the back of the APC. It was a smell that took him back to boyhood, to days of hot rods and drag strips, when his biggest worries had been whether he would have a date for Saturday, could he afford a new clutch for his dune buggy, would his pulled muscle be all right for the game Friday night. He worked his scar-puckered shoulder gingerly and found he could almost touch the back of his head. He was glad he could still remember the boy he once had been, but it was a distant memory, more like something he had read than a life he once lived. And the concentrated intensity of combat that he and his men had lived with since August made even the events of Firebreak, when the Soviets rolled across eastern Germany, seem remote, if too far from unreal. Tag was ready for this to be over.

Prentice saw him approaching and came to meet Tag.

"How's it going, Chuck?" Tag said.

"We've got all the ammo and personal gear passed out, and as soon as the jay kays are through, I've got another hundred and fifty gallons of fuel for the No Slack Too," Prentice said. "Any fresh thoughts on our next move?"

Tag shook his head. "Not really," he said. "I've got Tutti setting up to monitor all the satellite data we can get. Meanwhile, I want you and Giesla and Krager and me to take a look at the map."

The two men walked back to Prentice's Bradley, found Giesla and Gaylord Krager, and moved off into a small clearing nearby, taking with them an acetate-covered map from the possibles box on Giesla's commando vehicle. Tag spread the map on the ground, and they all hunkered on their heels around it.

"Okay," Tag began, "what we're looking for is someplace that will serve as a base camp and give us quick-strike capability to any of Ivan's most likely areas of movement. With the reinforced French divisions in the Black Forest, I don't see any need to burn fuel by trying to cover that base. Tell me if you think I'm wrong, but I'm saying that our job is still here in the Jura, to keep Ivan south of us. The First Guards aren't going to try to wind the whole army through the dead zone. Their best bet would be to gain the crest of the mountains and beat it back east. They'd still have to negotiate the hot strip between here and the mineworks, but that's a lot less radiation to dodge than anywhere else. It leaves us the high ground and a hell of a lot less area to cover. Gaylord, you're the devil's advocate; what do you think?"

The grizzled Ranger shifted on his hams and rubbed the stubble of his beard with the back of one hand while he studied the map.

"Well," he said at last, "given our orders, we don't have many choices, and I can't argue with what you say, Max. Sorry. But I think here"—he pointed to a small town farther west along the crest of the Jura—"is our best bet for a base camp. We can't leave ourselves too far from the French flank, in case Ivan is playing some kind of double-reverse psychology—you know, thinking we won't believe he is dumb enough to do the dumbest thing he can. But you're right about him not trying to break back through to the west. The line of least resistance is still here, along the crest of the Jura. One possibility is a fake toward the Black Forest, drawing some of our people back there, then a wheeling movement and a dash east."

Giesla said, "He is right, Max. Even with all the current intelligence Colonel Barlow provided, there is still nothing clear in the Soviet intentions. But the change in our status from reconnaissance to an attack group means something, perhaps that SACEUR does not expect the First Guards to wait on fate and politicians. We cannot leave ourselves out of position to support the French flank."

Tag nodded. "Yeah," he said. "Yeah, there's not much else for it, I guess. We've been a long way from the barn before. The orders stand. We'll bivouac here until morning, unless something happens to change plans, then move out for the village. Any questions?"

There were not, and the meeting broke up. Tag was halfway across the wooded ridge, headed for the No Slack Too, when he met Ham Jefferson running at a lope.

"Hey, boss," the gunner said breathlessly, "you'd better come see what Fruits has got on the screens."

Tag broke into a sprint.

Yeshev smiled and waved at the commander of one of the two T-80Bs he had dispatched with the First Battalion, his countenance belying his anxiety. He had played too much chess and sparred with Butcher Boy too many times to be sanguine about the chances two rooks and a rank of pawns would have against a mobile queen flanked by aggressive knights. He knew his best hope lay in luring the American into the heart of the board, where numbers could be as telling as mobility. And even at that, this was not endgame, merely a gambit, an exchange of pieces in the greater game. Nor was this chess. It was more like those video games the students at the war college were so fond of, the games in which the powers and abilities of a player could change magically and unbeknownst to the others.

Yeshev's confidence that the T-80B was a match for any NATO armor had been badly shaken by Butcher Boy's dash through the heart of the First Guards Army a month ago, although he drew the best face possible on the ambush that had put the American out of action these past few weeks. The low-slung black tank with the bristling weapons deck should never have escaped the pounding it received. And now, as well, he had to factor in the variables presented by the new design of Bradley that could withstand a medium antitank cannon. And he had to do it with dwindling supplies of everything except orders.

The smile fell from Yeshev's face as he watched the last of the battalion move past him. He turned to reenter the operations bunker and came face-to-face with Major Nikolai Viktor standing in the door.

"Why so glum, Comrade Colonel," Viktor asked sweetly, not disguising the satisfaction he felt at his commander's clear concern.

Yeshev cocked one eyebrow and said, "What—caught between the fire and the furnace, without resupply, the target of a vindictive NATO general who wants our skins, and given orders to do with less what we could not do with more—why, what could be better, Nikolai?"

"You do not sound as though you have complete and total confidence in the wisdom of our leaders, comrade," Viktor said, his voice oily with sarcasm and ominous in its implied threat of denunciation.

Anger boiled in Yeshev's ears. "Nikolai," he said evenly, "we may outwit Butcher Boy, we may even destroy him, but this game is not ours to win. We are

playing now for a stalemate, and you may tell your
keepers that I said it."

He brushed Major Viktor aside and ducked through
the door of the bunker.

Tag studied the VLD screen from his commander's
seat inside the No Slack Too and outlined an area of
the display with his light stylus. The screen winked
and the designated sector leapt to fill it.

"Fruits," Tag said, "where'd you say these pictures
were coming from?"

"LandSat North and dat geosynchronous Navy bird,"
Fruits Tutti said from the turret terminal, where he
was feverishly keying instructions into his custom
software. "Bad fuggin' angles, but—wait, I 'bout got
it—dere."

The image on the VLD folded over itself once,
causing Tag to blink and turn away, then the two
ghosts melded together and sharpened into a picture
of almost photographic clarity.

"Holy fuckin' moly," Tag said. "Must be fifty,
sixty pieces of armor in that column. You see 'em,
Ham?"

Ham Jefferson, sitting in the driver's seat next to
Tag, looked at his smaller liquid-crystal display and
said, "If you say so. Man, they go plumb off my
screen. Can you make out what they are, boss?"

"I'd say at least half are MBTs. The rest could be
2S-9s or something that size, anyway. Aw, shit, I'm
losing them. Fruits, can you get this back in focus?"

"Sorry, Captain Max," the loader said. "We lost da
LandSat. I'll hafta wait for the next pass. I can maybe
get a radar overhead at seventeen-hundred hours from
da Night Owl."

"Okay, Fruits. Thanks."

Tag switched off his screen and sat back in his chair. After a moment he said, "Fruits, can your program give any sort of projection on Ivan's likely routes, just from what we saw?"

"Yeah. Yeah. Gimme a minute."

"Staff Sergeant Jefferson," Tag said in a stage whisper, "remind me to have Sergeant Tutti court-martialed and shot."

"My pleasure, Captain Tag," the gunner said.

"Hey, fug you guys," Tutti muttered. "I got a war to fight."

In a few moments, Tag saw red lines stippling across his VLD, and Tutti said, "Dere, but it ain't nothin' you wouldn'ta guessed."

Fruits was right. Tag studied the projected routes, their probabilities reflected by the density of the lines, and found no surprises. The most likely object for the battalion was the village below them—or something on the route to it, at least.

"Fruits," he said, "give me ETAs for them to these coordinates." He marked four points along the line with his light stylus, and in seconds had his answers in the readout window along the left side of the screen. It would be morning at the earliest before the main body of the Soviet column could reach them, and well after dark before it reached any jumping off point for an alternative destination.

Tag switched off the VLD and said, "Okay, you guys carry on. I'll be back in a while."

Then he was out of the No Slack Too and hurrying through the timber back to the Jagd Kommandos' positions, where he found Giesla and her top sergeant, Mathias Betcher, and quickly outlined the developing situation to them.

Giesla stood back from the map they had spread

on the possibles box on the back of her vehicle and tapped her temple. "This is all very hasty," she said. "From what you describe, Max, it does not sound like a typical movement or even a planned one. If our intelligence is only approximately accurate, they are deploying nearly half of their remaining antitank reconnaissance unit but none of their infantry units."

"Right," Tag said. "It doesn't look like an assault, but that's too much armor for a patrol. It doesn't fit any scenario we expected, does it?"

"We need, perhaps, a closer look?" Betcher said, and Tag and Giesla both agreed.

"Mathias," said Giesla, "take Jan or Karl and move into position here, where they will either have to turn back west or commit toward us. Avoid contact, old friend. Just see what they do and bring it back to us at once."

Betcher showed his small, even teeth in what, for him, passed as a grin. "My pleasure, Lieutenant," he said, then turned away and bawled out for a driver.

Betcher was a good soldier, and Jan Metzger, the young Jagd Kommando who accompanied him, was the best of the rest, so they both thought very carefully about the orders Giesla had given them, about the distinction between "avoid contact" and "no contact." With two T-80Bs and a pair of 2S9 toy tanks in their sights, the Kommandos were as excited as boys with their first deer in the cross hairs.

They had arrived at their position well after dark but more than an hour before the Soviet column appeared, and they had watched through their night-vision scopes while the column halted, men got out of the tanks to talk, and all but four reversed their direction and sped back the way that they came. The two remaining main battle tanks and the two pieces of light antitank armor deployed themselves on a hillside opposite the Jagd Kommandos' position, from which they could cover the T-intersection, where a fire trail met the secondary road on which the column had been traveling. As each piece of Russian armor took up its ambush position—for Betcher could see clearly what they intended—the Jagd Kommandos plotted it on the computer that controlled the rack of antitank guided missiles on top of the commando vehicle. They had four of the AT-20 Brancher missiles and one tank for each of them.

"Jan," Mathias Betcher said softly, "I think we have no choice."

Jan nodded. "Yes, Sergeant," he said. "There is no way we could avoid contact, although we did try."

"Fire in volley," Betcher said.

The four missiles leapt from the rack in unison deafening Jan and Betcher with the scream of their propellant. The two toy tanks exploded like over-heated aerosol cans, twisted sheets of their light armor spinning crazily through the treetops away from the canopies of flame that enveloped the 2S9s. One of of the T-80Bs was situated with its nose pointing down the slope, and it took a hit on the thinly armored roof of its turret. The resulting explosion inside blew out all three hatches before igniting the ammunition magazine with a force that tore through the engine compartment and blasted back the rear deck, exposing the naked, burning guts of the tank. The second T-80B was struck on the turret just below the gun mantle. The missile did not penetrate the armor, but it warped the main tube and rendered it useless, while the men inside were knocked unconscious by the concussion.

"Go," Betcher said.

Jan spun their gun buggy in reverse, the honeycomb tires spinning rooster tails of forest mulch as he slammed the synchromesh transmission into first gear and shot back into the woods.

Fifteen kilometers to the west, the commander of Yeshev's Second Battalion was already looking for a place of concealment before first light.

Giesla's voice woke Tag.

"Max," she said, "Mathias and Jan have returned, and they have some very interesting information."

Five minutes later Tag was standing in the dappled moonlight beneath the trees listening to Betcher's report. When he had finished, Giesla said to her burly NCO, "So, there was no avoiding the contact, Mathias?"

Betcher pulled his face in a long, unconvincing look of contrition. "No," he said. "It was beyond our control. But," he added, struggling to keep the satisfaction from his voice, "it was a most lovely sight."

"Betcher," Tag said, "you are an evil sonofabitch, and I'm sure you couldn't help it. Good work."

"Yes, Mathias," said Giesla, "I am certain that you followed your orders to the letter. Get some sleep now. We have an early start."

When the two Jagd Kommandos were out of earshot, Giesla turned to Tag and said, "What do you make of it, Max?"

Tag shrugged, his mind still thick with sleep. "I dunno, Gies. Dunno. We'll get the Early Bird pictures in about three hours. Maybe they'll tell us something. Whatever it is Ivan's up to, it's something we didn't expect. Maybe it's that big push Barlow hinted about, but I dunno. I'm gonna sleep on it."

Giesla kissed him softly on the jaw.

"Both of us, Max," she said. "Or perhaps N. Sain will have a vision."

Yeshev could not sleep. He was in the operations bunker, drinking strong tea and smoking cardboard-filtered cigarettes, when the distress call came in from the T-80B that had survived the Jagd Kommando ambush. He ordered a detachment from First Battalion to return and escort the crippled tank home, then, at last, went to his own bunker for a few hours' fitful sleep. At least now he knew that Butcher Boy could see them during the day. Although raised an atheist, Yeshev found himself mumbling prayers for his men in Second Battalion and for the half-dozen T-80Bs with it. Without them, he had no illusions about his chances. He prayed that the American could not see at night, for now they were playing blindman's bluff.

6

The first satellite photos came in at 0610, and what they showed puzzled Tag. The images of the Soviet positions, particularly of the antitank regiment, were perfect—except that there were not enough tanks. The emplacements were half deserted. Yesterday, there had been more than a hundred pieces of armor, half of them moving out toward Tag's position. These, he knew from Betcher's intelligence, had turned back. But this morning, the pictures did not confirm that they had ever arrived at the Soviet emplacement or that they were anywhere else within SOUTHAG.

Ham Jefferson, crouched in the space between the driver's seat and the commander's chair, scowled at the VLD and said, "You suppose they dug in, boss, maybe moved under camouflage?"

"I don't know, Ham," Tag said, "but I don't think so. There just hasn't been that much activity around there until yesterday. If they did it, they did it all last night. No, there's something else going on."

Tag thought a minute, then had Fruits superimpose yesterday's pictures on the current ones.

Holy shit! Tag thought as the two images came into register. The positions that had been left empty when the column left the Soviet position were occupied now. It was the others that were vacated. The rest of the antitank regiment had moved out while the first column was returning—but where had they gone?

Tag met briefly with Giesla and Prentice to tell them what he didn't know, and to pass the word that the raiders would travel at long intervals, with gun buggies at point and on extended flanks.

"The only thing we know for sure," he said to the others before they moved out, "is that we've got maybe a battalion of bad guys that we can't locate, and I don't want them to find us first. Let's move fast, but let's move smart."

At just after 0700 the raiders rolled down the ridge and took to the road below at high speed, all defensive systems activated. It was colder here in the morning shadows of the mountain, and an early November frost lay heavily on the berm along the road. The air was sharp and stung Tag's cheeks as he rode in the hatch, steering by feel and turning things over in his mind. But by the time the frost had burned away and they had come in sight of the village that was their objective, things were no clearer to him than they had been when he first received the satellite data. The image Fruits Tutti had once used of feeling your way along a dark hall, looking for an open door and praying it wasn't an elevator shaft, came back to Tag as he brought the column to a halt and ordered the vehicles into the woods on either side of the road.

Tag climbed stiffly out of the hatch, favoring his shoulder, slid down the glacis of the No Slack Too, and crossed the road to Prentice's Bradley.

"Chuck," he said, "get your glasses and come with me. I want to have a peek at our new home from here, then you can send in a squad to check it out."

"Be right with you," Prentice said.

The two men recrossed the road to the high side and walked a few hundred meters through the woods, until they had a clear view of the hamlet. Sitting on the forest floor, Tag steadied his elbows on his knees and adjusted the focus of his binoculars. Beside him, Prentice did the same.

The place was hardly a village at all, and the shelling it had taken during the initial Soviet assault weeks before had been heavy. There were perhaps a hundred homes and buildings, mostly wood and mostly single-story. The whole thing would have fit easily in the parking lot of a shopping mall. The majority of the structures had been damaged by artillery, and subsequent fires had destroyed several of them on the south and east sides of town. Near the center of the village, where a better road crossed north–south, the shops and public buildings had been largely spared.

"Looks quiet to me, Max," Prentice said.

"Yep," Tag agreed. "A real ghost town. Go ahead and send your people in, Chuck. I'll position N. Sain and the No Slack Too to cover 'em from here."

While Prentice briefed Villalobos and the men of his squad, Tag moved his tank and the other Bradley into position and ordered the Jagd Kommandos and the remainder of the Rangers to form a hasty perimeter to the flanks and rear. Birds sang in the bright blue sky, and Tag thought: *Christ, you're getting cautious in your old age.*

In a week, he would be thirty-one.

In less than a half hour, a runner from the patrol reported back with an "all clear," and by midmorning, Tag's raiders had invested the village.

Tag put Prentice and Krager in charge of establishing perimeter positions for the Rangers, dispatched two of the Jagd Kommando vehicles to cover the approaches on the north–south road, and positioned the Bradleys on the east and west, leaving the No Slack Too and one gun buggy as reinforcements. In the center of the hamlet, he found for his headquarters an intact two-story building, once the municipal offices, and behind it a garage and shed that housed a snowplow, two road graders, a tractor, and the single local bus, where the XM-F4 and Giesla's Kommando vehicle could be held in reserve and out of sight. He gave Fruits and Ham—the best scroungers he had ever known—the responsibility of surveying the hamlet for anything the raiders could use.

Before evening chow, the unit was right at home. Ham and Fruits, using the tractor from the shed to pull a flatbed trailer, had collected an impressive inventory of goods. In addition to the fuel and lubricants in the garage, they had cumshawed cases of canned goods, beer, and liquor from the local food stores, along with candy, cigarettes, socks, underwear, toothpaste, soap, tapes and CDs and players, batteries, flashlights, a portable generator and light system, several pairs of binoculars, fifty decks of cards, enough duct tape to patch the *Titanic*, a couple of elegant high-powered sporting rifles with telescopic sights, more than a mile of electrical wire, two fifty-pound boxes of commercial-grade plastic explosives, and the ugliest dog Tag had ever seen.

The animal was a tall, skinny, mottled-gray beast—part-mastiff and part God-knows-what, by the look of him—with a massive head and jaws, mismatched eyes, a penis sheath as big as a donkey's, and something of an attitude. Fruits had already christened the dog Porno.

"I'm not even going to ask how you managed to find any PE in this burg," Tag said, "but where the fuck did that mongrel come from—and why, for Pete's sake?" He was recalling Fruits's palpitating fear of the two shepherds at the animal clinic that the raiders had once used as a hospital. Hell, Tutti had always been afraid of dogs.

During Tag's railing, Porno shifted warily from side to side a few feet behind Fruits, trying to keep something between himself and Tag. The dog kept his ears back, and his eyes cut around the motor pool to be sure no one was sneaking up on him.

"Hey, Captain," Fruits whined, "it ain't my fault. He adopted me. I can't help it none."

"He just likes the way you smell," Ham Jefferson said. "Thinks you're one of his own."

"Aw, fug you. The mothafugger's hungry, dat's all."

"Jeez," Tag said in exasperation, "what the hell is he anyway?" But as he began to step past Tutti for a closer look, the dog contracted into a crouch, showed a double row of young, strong teeth, and began to growl a rumbling growl deep in his chest. Tag froze.

"All right," he said. "Feed the sonofabitch, then, and see if you can improve his attitude. But he's your dog, Mr. Tutti, and if he causes any trouble, he's a dead dog. Understand?"

Fruits nodded mutely, and Porno growled again, edging up beside the loader's knee and drooling from the corners of his dewlaps.

Tag turned and walked back inside the headquarters building, one ear cocked for sounds of paws coming at his back.

While Ham and Fruits had been scrounging, Tag, Giesla, and Krager had been setting up a command center. On the ground floor of the building, in what had been the village offices, they had installed a wireless field telephone connected to the Ranger outposts ringing the village, and turned the private offices into billets. On the second story, four gable windows provided unobstructed views of every quadrant and served as an observation post from which Tag could see his entire position and all the approaches to it.

Despite all this, Tag was not at ease with his situation. Accustomed to being on the move, he did not feel quite right or at all safe being stuck in a fixed position, however homey or secure it seemed—especially with half a hundred pieces of Soviet armor on the prowl. And he didn't want his men to lose their edge either. He needed to call in Prentice, set a schedule of patrols, and establish some forward listening posts. But first, he decided, he needed to let off some nervous energy, and he set off alone, on foot, to inspect the perimeter.

Tag had only an hour or so of good light, so he walked briskly, trying to ignore the creeping chill of evening that was causing his wounded shoulder to stiffen. He found Gaylord Krager overseeing the distribution of the personal items that Ham and Fruits had scrounged, and he invited Krager to come with him on the inspection of the Ranger positions.

Sergeant Dunn, the former OED specialist in charge of the first squad, had the southern arc of the perimeter, and Tag and Krager found him discussing the deployment of claymore mines and listening devices with the Jagd Kommando Jan.

"Everything in order, Sergeant Dunn?" Tag asked.

Dunn returned a cocky grin and said, "Yes, sir. We're spread thin as deli ham, but ain't nobody gonna slip in on us. We got two rows of claymores and range stakes every fifty meters. Me and Jan here was just discussin' response procedures."

"Where are your M-Sixties, Dunn?" Krager said.

"We got one covering that defilade over there to the right"—he pointed toward a tree line that followed a wet-weather stream about three hundred meters away—"and the other set up to cover the left flank and support Jan here if anything comes up the road."

Tag nodded in approval. "Good work," he said. "Pull four of your people and have them ready in thirty minutes for maps and briefing. They'll be running a night patrol."

"You got 'em, Captain," Dunn replied.

Tag and Krager continued their inspection, pulling another four men from Villalobos's squad for patrol duty, then returned to the headquarters, where Fruits was processing the last of the daytime satellite data, and Porno lay curled on a plush-covered couch nearby. The dog raised his head and growled at Tag.

"Did you feed that animal, Tutti?" Tag asked irritably.

"Yeah," Fruits said, not looking up from the computer keyboard, "gave him some MREs. He's real mellowed out now. Would ya believe it, Captain; dey had a Nextphase seven-seven-two right here in dis dinky joint. We're all patched in to the Too's system. Getya anything ya want from de comfort of your own office."

"Well, get me the latest from the Night Owl, then."

"Comin' up."

Fruits stroked the keys, and the color monitor began overlaying designs, while the printer on the stand beside it hummed a laser-pixel tune.

Tag scanned the monitor as the printed image scrolled from the platen. When the printer fell silent, he ripped the hard copy from its carriage and compared it to the picture on the screen.

Tag scowled and sucked his cheek. "Fruits," he said, "get me enlargements on a one-klick grid of every inch of country between here and Ivan's positions. There's got to be something we're not seeing.

"Gaylord," he said, turning to Krager, "pass the word to Lieutenant Prentice that I want Dunn's patrol to extend four or five klicks. Be sure they have a radio with burp capabilities. They may have to stay out a day or two. The other patrol will sweep north and east at about one klick out, then bring them in."

"I'm on my way," Krager said. He snarled at Porno as he left the room. The dog ignored him.

Tag turned and spoke to Ham, who was sprawled in a sprung waiting-room chair, reading a paperback novel with a cover that included fire-belching machine guns, four grime-and-blood-covered soldiers of fortune, artillery air bursts, and a woman with her shirt torn open, exposing large, firm, pink-nippled breasts.

"Hambone," he said, "I hate to interrupt a man who's trying to improve his mind, but get off your sorry ass and go find Lieutenant Ruther for me."

Ham stood and tossed the book on the sunken seat of the chair. "Just when I's gettin' to the good part too," he muttered.

By the time Ham returned with Giesla—who stopped to pat Porno on the head, the dog thumping his knout-size tail on the sofa and licking her hand—Fruits had the printouts ready that Tag had asked for. Tag spread them on a desk and all four gathered around.

"I don't know what we're looking for," Tag said, "but there's got to be something that'll give us a clue to where those other tanks have gone. Fruits, you and Ham start at the Soviet positions and work through the pictures coming toward us. Gies and I will work from the other end."

Using sheet-magnifiers that Tag had found in a drafting office on the second floor, they leaned over the desk and began studying the blowups of the satellite photos. Krager returned with a billycan of coffee for them, then sat in silence by the field phone, waiting for something to happen.

"Bing-fuckin' -o," Fruits Tutti said, twenty minutes into their work. "I think we got a winner, Captain Max."

Tag moved around the desk to the end Fruits and Ham shared. "Show me," he said.

Fruits centered the magnifying sheet over the picture. "Have a look," he said.

It took Tag only a moment to recognize a symmetrical pattern of contrasting shades: two staggered rows of dark mottles among the rich, dying colors of autumn, green against yellows and reds. He counted more than thirty on this sheet alone.

"They continue on the next grid?" he asked.

"Sure do, boss," Ham said, sliding another sheet to him. "Look close, and you don't even need the enlarger."

Sure enough, Tag could, now that he knew what he was looking for, see the same pattern continued on the next photo in the sequence.

"What is it, Max?" Giesla asked as she stepped around the desk to his side.

"I think we found our missing tanks," Tag said. "I think the season changed on 'em, and they couldn't change their cammo. Thank God for ol' Ivan going by the book. If it hadn't been for the pattern, we might have missed 'em. But if that isn't a column of Soviet armor in concealment, I'll eat your helmet.

"Gaylord," he called to Krager, whose interest had picked up the moment he heard Fruits's sing out, "are those patrols ready yet?"

"They oughtta be," Krager replied.

"Well, get ahold of Dunn's bunch and tell them not to budge until they hear from me. Looks like we may have something for them."

Krager picked up the field phone, and Tag spread out a topo map on a desk adjacent to the one with the photos.

"Okay, Fruits," he said, "show me what grid that is over here."

In a matter of minutes, Tag and Fruits had pinpointed the location of the Soviet formation, calculated its speed and direction from its base position, and projected its movement along three possible contingency routes, any of which would bring the column within cannon shot of the village by daybreak.

Calculating how fast his own night patrols could move, Tag said to Krager, "Gaylord, tell Villalobos's herd to hold up too. I think we're scratching the local patrol."

At 2010, an eight-man Ranger patrol, led by Sergeant Dunn, left the village, moving south-southeast, with orders to recon and, possibly, interdict and harass a suspected Soviet armored column, and to report either by radio burp or in person no later than 0400 the next morning. Tag put his base on full alert.

Yeshev had, at last, slept, but when he awoke it was with a hammering heart and sweat rolling like ball bearings off his chest. He threw back the flap of his heavy sleeping bag and sat on the edge of the cot in his bunker, fighting against hyperventilation and a sudden attack of shivering.

In his dream he had been walking along a familiar hall in the Kremlin, where the army kept offices. The smells of tobacco and janitorial soap were mixed with the fluorescent odor of ozone, and a green, undersea light suffused the dream. Each door he tried was locked, and he was anxious not to be late for whatever it was he had come there for. Suddenly one of the doors opened at his touch, and he rushed into the green fog only to find there was nothing beneath his feet. He was falling, faster and faster, flapping his arms to fly—and then he awoke.

It was not the dream that had frightened him, however, but the realization that had come upon him as he fell. Because Butcher Boy was regular army and an American, not an indigenous guerrilla, Yeshev had been ignoring the lessons of guerrilla warfare learned at such high cost by the Americans in Vietnam and by his own people in Afghanistan more than twenty years before. He had not equated what he was doing with the tactic of stumbling around in an enemy's territory to invite a strike, then hoping to prevail by superior firepower. But it could easily turn into that. His sole consolation was that, so far, Butcher Boy had not responded to the night maneuvers. Perhaps it was just a silly dream.

As he lit one of his harsh, cardboard-filtered cigarettes, Yeshev's hand shook.

Traveling by a series of secondary roads and well-worn fire trails, Dunn and his patrol covered their first ten kilometers in less than two hours, before he called a break and recalculated their optional objectives on his map. The men were fresh and tough, but if they missed the Soviet column, there would be no catching up and no chance to slow its advance. Even these Rangers could not run down a T-80. But the more Dunn looked at the map and the terrain, the more convinced he became that Ivan's best alternatives were to head directly toward the village or to swing to the west. And if that was the case, there was only one place where the Soviets could make their move, an intersection of the main north–south road and a secondary road about fifteen klicks from the village and less than five from where he now was.

No guts, no glory, Dunn told himself, and he ordered the men to saddle up.

Major Yuri Gerisimov, the commander of Yeshev's Second Battalion, had a decision to make. His training in antitank battle tactics and reconnaissance had not included any classes on independent thinking, but as his column approached the T-intersection, he was faced with that prospect. Butcher Boy had no history of going to ground, at least not in built-up areas, so there was little likelihood he would have invested the village. And Gerisimov's orders were to seek out Butcher Boy and destroy him. But he was almost to the point of no return for his fuel supplies. There were, perhaps, fuel stores available in the village, and with them he could extend his range and his mission. On the other hand, if Butcher Boy had fallen for the feint toward the Black Forest, he would be farther west.

After much anguish, Yuri Gerisimov made a daring decision: he would split his command.

Dunn was getting worried. The undergrowth was thick and the erosion gullies rugged, and moving cross-country at night was proving slower than he had calculated. It was becoming clear to him that they could not reach the intersection in time to be sure of intercepting the armored column.

Dunn called a brief halt, took out his map, and illuminated it with a red-filtered light. The Rangers could cut more than a klick off their march by going due west and hitting the primary road between the intersection and the village. That way, even if he didn't spot the column, he would know where it had gone.

Gerisimov stopped his T-80B at the intersection and got out to personally brief each tank crew and to direct their deployment. The detachment to the west was to proceed another ten kilometers, before turning back north and converging on the village from the west, unless they or the remainder of the battalion made contact first.

Once the decision was made, Gerisimov felt elated, certain he was in command of the situation. Moving these metal monsters at his sole command, like a chess master manipulating his pieces, gave the Soviet major a rush of confidence and resolution. Butcher Boy was in the hot oil now.

Dunn could not see his men in the darkness, only the ghostly plumes of their labored breath condensing in the cold night air from behind the trees and boulders where they lay in ambush for the Soviet tanks that they all hoped would come. There had been no need for orders once they reached the road; every man knew what he had to do. Dunn had made a quick recon of the road and found no sign that the tanks had passed, and when he had finished, the ambush was in place, with one man positioned two hundred meters down the road to get a gander at the length of the column as it passed into the kill zone.

The Rangers shivered in anticipation. Beside each of them lay two light antitank weapons, their tubes extended and opened, their pins pulled, ready to fire. The men rehearsed their exfiltration routes in their minds, anxious to hit and run. They hadn't long to wait.

Dunn heard the growl of approaching armor and snapped his night-vision goggles into place. Through the red cast of the glasses, he saw a wedge of three T-80s leading the column, followed by a staggered file of smaller 2S9s, with the vague, larger shapes of MBTs looming behind.

Dunn waited until he judged the lead element of the column to be abreast of the men to his right, then he sighted in his first LAW and triggered the ambush.

Within seconds of Dunn's mashing the bar trigger on his rocket launcher, the other six tubes in the ambush released their rounds, ripping the night with explosions and drowning the noise of motors and clanking treads. The flash of exploding rockets was followed by a staccato of secondary reports from inside the punctured 2S9s. His own first target flashed flame from split seams in its armor, while Dunn snatched up his second LAW and zeroed in on the rear of one of the main battle tanks to his right. He steadied his sights, fired, and watched as the red-orange eye of burning propellant flew from him and disappeared in the greater glare of the warhead that struck the T-80B's track skirt.

He had no leisure to evaluate the hit. Dunn threw the expended tube aside and sprinted at a crouch into the safety of the forest shadows. Within minutes, all his men were assembled at the rendezvous and moving at route step back toward the village. Dunn looked at the illuminated dial of his watch: 0215. They had plenty of time to get back to headquarters before the 0400 deadline, and the fourteen confirmed hits that his patrol had recorded ought to hold Ivan for a while.

Tag was awake and pacing the floor when word came from the perimeter that Dunn's patrol was in. Porno, who had refused to relinquish his place on the sofa, followed Tag warily with his eyes, growling and farting, while Tag spoke hurriedly on the field phone before rousting Ham and Fruits and bolting out the door to go meet Dunn and his men.

"Wait a minute," Tag said, interrupting Dunn's recitation of the patrol report. "You mean that by your count there were only two dozen pieces of armor in the column?"

"Right, Captain," said Dunn, "and we zapped more'n half of 'em. Those toy tanks went up like fireworks."

"And you made a clean break?"

"I'm telling you, sir, they never knew what hit 'em," Dunn insisted. "It was wham, bam, and scram."

Yuri Gerisimov saw a ring of light expanding in the dark center of his vision, like a ripple on a pond that disappeared at the edges. Then another and another, until his sight began to clear, if not his head. He felt heat on one cheek and biting cold on the other. He tried to turn toward the heat, and pain dug at the back of his skull. It was another moment before he realized he was lying on the ground.

Shaking his head, he pushed himself up on one elbow and blinked to focus his eyes. Tanks, his iron chessmen, were burning all along the road, and his own T-80B sat not far away, collapsed on one side where a LAW rocket had shattered its track, the glacis scorched from the impact that had knocked him unconscious. Gerisimov struggled to his feet and lurched among the running, shouting men, crying out for his tank commanders.

If Butcher Boy is in that village, he thought, *I will not leave a stick standing.*

Once he had regained his senses and tallied the damage to his unit, Gerisimov had gathered enough presence of mind to recall the tanks enveloping to the west and to organize a patrol to reconnoiter the village on foot.

At 0420, out beyond the perimeter, a Ranger at a listening post equipped with electronic ears heard the soft rustle of leaves made by the Soviet foot patrol. He tensed and listened. It was a small unit. He scanned the woods with the directional audio pickup and heard nothing else, then keyed the handset on his radio in a coded pattern to indicate what he had heard.

Tag got the message and immediately called for a changing of watches at the perimeter posts and also had the Bradleys rev up their engines, as if charging batteries.

Thirty minutes later, another listening post reported the patrol leaving the vicinity. Tag turned and smiled to those with him in the command center.

"Okay," he said, "listen up, folks. We're about to have some fun."

Yeshev took the news of the ambush stoically. Gerisimov had not indicated how bad the ambush had been, but he did report that he had Butcher Boy's position and was closing on it.

Yeshev blew cigarette smoke from his nostrils and snatched at it with his hand. He opened his fist and stared glumly at the empty palm, reflecting that the only way to capture smoke was from above.

7

Within twenty minutes of learning that the Soviet patrol had left the area, Tag had his Rangers in the Bradleys and all of the vehicles moving out of town to the east. He led them as far as the wooded hillside from which he and Prentice had first viewed the hamlet, and there Tag threw his unit into a tight perimeter, no more than fifty meters across. The Rangers took position on the ground, but the troop ramps on the Bradleys remained open, all engines idling.

Tag kept his eyes glued to the IR commander's scope inside the *No Slack Too*, scanning the periphery of the village for movement, while Fruits monitored the Phalanx radar. Porno, whom Tag had found already in the tank when they left the village (Fruits denying any notion of how he got there), squatted in the driver's seat, his forefeet on the floor, and emitted the stifling farts that only MREs can produce.

Tag hit the "fresh air" switch on the ventilator system. The calf-size mongrel was less than a minor distraction to him at the moment. Right now, Tag was absorbed in trying to deduce Ivan's whereabouts, since he was nearly certain that it was the No Slack Too and the raider unit—not the Black Forest—that was the object of Soviet desires.

Gerisimov's crews had worked furiously while the foot patrol was out, and by the time it returned they had two of the T-80Bs and two of the less badly damaged 2S9s ready to fight, reducing Gerisimov's losses to one MBT and eight of the toy tanks. The return of the second column swelled his force to more than forty pieces of armor, and Gerisimov found anger replacing the battered confusion he had suffered immediately following the ambush.

The patrol confirmed that the NATO unit was in the village, holding a thin perimeter to slack security, obviously feeling safely hidden and taking an armed holiday.

Gerisimov re-formed his column with his twenty-three main battle tanks, including the T80Bs, in the van. Two kilometers from the village, the 2S9s would commence a rocket barrage, fired from their smooth-bore 120mm multiguns, while the heavier armor swept forward to overrun the Allied position in the resulting confusion. Then the light tanks would circle the flanks and cut off any fleeing survivors.

It did not occur to Gerisimov that he might have lost the element of surprise.

At false dawn, thirty minutes before shooting light, Fruits Tutti croaked over the intercom, "Incomin'."

Seconds later, Tag saw the perimeter of the village leap into flame, ringed by air bursts from the Soviet rockets. Before the afterimages could fade from his retinas, a second volley of rockets fell concentrically within the circle of the first, these exploding on impact among the outlying houses. Then the explosive impacts fell more raggedly, as the Soviet gunners walked fire across the heart of the village, demolishing the buildings that had been Tag's headquarters less than an hour before.

"Jeez," Fruits said, "must be more'n twenty tubes out dere." He looked down from his seat in the turret at Porno, who had himself turned and looked up when Fruits began to speak. "Now," Tutti said to the dog, "ain'tya glad you came?"

Porno ripped another braying fart and thumped his tail.

"Mr. Tutti," Tag said, "we are going to have a serious talk about you and your soul mate here when this is done."

Tag could hear Fruits muttering over the intercom, whining up for a reply, when the barrage suddenly ceased and a crescent of Soviet main battle tanks broke from the woods surrounding the village on the south and west, their cannons blazing away at anything left standing. As they closed on the smoking remains of his former headquarters, Tag saw a loose column of 2S9s come into his field of vision at high speed and peel back to the east, in his direction.

He shouted out the hatch to the Rangers, "Stand by. Pass the word. Possible bogeys."

But the toy tanks ignored the east–west road, rolled across it, and sealed the backside of the assault. Tag could tell from their erratic, too-cautious movements that Ivan was confused. A quick nose count told Tag that all or nearly all of the Soviet armor that Dunn had reported was in the village, all in his sights.

Tag weighed his situation quickly, trying to envision his operational options, and as quickly reached a decision. Gambling that the Soviets were occupied with their own confusion, he keyed the TacNet and said, "Meat Grinder, this is Butcher Boy. Withdraw at once to Square One." He was ordering the Jagd Kommandos back to the mineworks, beyond the nuclear-strike line and out of the area of operations. "I say again, withdraw to Square One. Out."

Tag had not called for a response; he did not want to explain anything to Giesla. But before he had composed his orders in his mind for Prentice and N. Sain, Giesla was outside his hatch, speaking to him with barely contained distemper.

"Max," she said sharply, "what are you doing?"

He stood in the hatch and put his face close to hers. "Listen, Gies," he said rapidly, "there's no time for details. I'm gonna try to lead Ivan back from here, and I may have to use the red zones for cover. That's no place for your buggies. Be a soldier and follow your orders. And when you get back, be a vamp and see if you can get Barlow to get us some air cover."

Giesla grabbed Tag on either side of his helmet and kissed him hard on the mouth. "Yes, sir," she said and slid down off the glacis.

Tag raised Prentice and N. Sain on the TacNet and ordered them to reload the Rangers and pull their Bradleys into positions where they could cover the village. The three Jagd Kommando gun buggies broke from the perimeter and sped to the east, soon lost from sight in the dawn light. By then, the Bradleys were in position, and Tag took the time to brief N. Sain and Prentice in person. He ran to each of the APCs and called their commanders out.

Standing between the Bradleys, with Prentice looking solemn and professional, and N. Sain shifting
anxiously from foot to foot, Tag said, "Okay, I've
sent the Kommandos back, because I don't know
what this may lead to, but it might be back into the
hot spots. Right now, I want to get Ivan away from
the crest and out from between us and the French
flank. We're gonna throw a few rounds at him and
then run. If we hit him too hard, I'm afraid they may
just reinforce and dig in. So, take good shots, but only
two—understand, N. Sain? just two?—then we haul
ass. You just follow me. Got it?"

Prentice only nodded, and N. Sain said, "O Avatar
of Ambush, I feel the fullness coming."

"Uh-huh," Tag grunted. "For right now, you go fill
your seat."

Back at his scope inside the No Slack Too, Tag
surveyed the village and marked two main battle
tanks for Ham's 120mm, then called up the area
map on his screen and began plotting their route.
When Prentice and N. Sain reported that they were
locked on targets, Tag gave the order to fire.

The scream of propellant from the Bradleys' missiles was lost in the bellow from the XM-F4's main
gun as it recoiled into its dampers twice in quick succession, releasing a pair of high-explosive rounds.

The missiles and the 120mm HEs tore a ragged
hole in the Soviet formation, and five more Communist tanks and crews died in the conflagration of
ordnance and fuel that boiled from their ranks. The
MBTs that Tag had targeted lost radio masts, snorkels,
and turret-mounted machine guns, but their improved
armor saved them from complete destruction. They
would still be able to fight—but fight wounded.

Another 2S9 survived when a whistling War Club went wide.

Tag did not stay in position long enough to record their hits. With Prentice's and N. Sain's almost-simultaneous announcements of "All away," Tag spun the No Slack Too around and lashed its turbines to life. The two Bradleys fell in behind, straining under their loads of troops to keep pace with the tank as they careened down the wooded slope and onto the road by which they had first arrived.

Return fire from the Soviet gunners was already ripping into the trees at the top of the slope when Tag hit the road. He flipped the "Smoke" switch on and off, squirting a billow of white from the rear of the XM-F4, not for concealment but to get the Soviets' attention, then led the Bradleys into the trees on the other side, still moving down-slope to the south-southeast.

Tag had his place in mind and kept up a hard pace for the Bradleys for a half hour until they reached it, the sharp crest of a narrow transverse ridge. Well wooded and with a command of the mountain to either side, the ridge would not allow anything to envelope on them and would admit only a single file of armor, if Ivan was in pursuit. By some careful jockeying, the Bradleys edged past the No Slack Too and took positions along their escape route to the south, where the transverse ridge rejoined the bulk of the Jura.

"Fruits," Tag said, "put your ears on. I'm activating the ADF."

With the audio-directional finder scanning for sounds of an enemy approach, Tag began feverish-ly composing a message to be burped to SACEUR via Barlow. His fingers flew across the keyboard of the computer, pausing only long enough for him to consider what sort of enticement it might take to get an air strike. One pass by stealth fighter bombers would effectively eliminate Ivan's antitank reconnaissance capabilities, and thus end any possible threat by the First Guards Army, scotch any attempt they might make at a breakout or against the French.

Tag rewrote his communication several times before he was satisfied that it said what he meant and could be contained in a one-second burp. He entered it for coding, waited for the confirmation, then keyed the radio. In seconds he had an acknowledgment and a coded request to stand by for a reply.

While Tag waited, fidgeting in his seat, Ham Jefferson said, "What's the skinny, bossman?"

"I'm trying to get Kettle to authorize a stealth strike, Hambone," Tag said. "If we could get that, I think it would put a cork in the bottle."

"SACEUR ain't never gonna give you no air strike," Ham said wearily. "Hell, we're not even here, s' far as the general's concerned."

"Yeah," Tag said, "but Ivan is. And these hills are getting a mite crowded, for my taste. I figure it's worth a shot."

Tag's computer beeped, and a row of block letters appeared on the screen: MESSAGE DESTROYED. END TRANSMISSION.

"What you got?" Ham asked.

"Bugger my boots," Tag said in disgust. "Got the shaft, is what I got, Ham."

"I's right again, huh?"

"Yeah, and I'm getting real sick of it. Hell, there won't even be any record of that little exchange."

"So, now what?" Ham said.

"Plan B."

"And what be Plan B?"

"I'm working on it, Ham," Tag said. "I'm working on it."

Major Gerisimov was using every strength he could muster to maintain his composure. He knew that his crews, already strained by being cut off and short of supplies, were not enjoying a surplus of confidence, especially not after being ambushed twice in one day. For that matter, neither was he. Here he was, actually in sight of Butcher Boy, and in too great a disarray to pursue. He had had the presence of mind to dispatch a troika of 2S9s after the fleeing American, but he knew they would serve more as security than as an attack unit. At least that would give him time to regroup his shattered ranks, try to scrounge for fuel, and devise some sort of plan. He wrestled with the idea of contacting Yeshev for orders, but his pride would not allow it.

In less than five hours, Gerisimov had lost almost half of his armor, including his own T-80B, and six more of his tanks were damaged.

Gerisimov quelled most of his indecision by taking personal charge of establishing fighting positions for his remaining effectives and pressing his junior officers into duty as scroungers. His head still throbbing from the concussions his tank had absorbed, Gerisimov kept moving among the smoking ruins of the village and his own tanks, ordering crews into position, pressing one of the standard T-80s into service as a bulldozer to create fighting positions in the rubble, and generally trying to keep his men whipped to a fighting pitch, while he tried to decide what to do next.

After more than an hour, Gerisimov had worked

himself out of job. No longer able to lose himself in details and unable to arrive at a military option he liked, he fell back on propaganda and began composing a message to Yeshev.

Yeshev returned the handset to the sergeant on radio watch in the bunker and turned to his operations officer.

"Well, Professor," he said to Minski, "it looks as though Major Gerisimov has had some success—if one can call catching the tiger by the tail a success."

"What did he say, Comrade Colonel?" Minski asked.

"Less than he means, I think," said Yeshev. "He reports two engagements—no details—and that he has taken the village where Butcher Boy was headquartered. He hints that he has neutralized the Jagd Kommando elements with Butcher Boy, and says that the American tank and the two APCs are hiding in the Jura south of the village. He wants air support."

"Air support!" Minski exclaimed. "Is the man drunk?"

"Worse," said Yeshev. "I think he may be right. Butcher Boy has already proven that he has aerial intelligence capacities. With that, his speed, and his armor, he can effectively neutralize our superior numbers and firepower. We have already seen that we cannot surround him on the ground. Our best hope to even the field is to cast a net over him, pin him down until Gerisimov can close and finish him off."

"And what will command say to all this?" Minski asked.

Yeshev shrugged. "That depends upon how important Butcher Boy really is to them. If they are poor gamblers, they will say yes."

"Yet you say that it might work? What is the fear?" Minski asked.

"No fear, Professor," said Yeshev, "only no point. Yes, we can destroy Butcher Boy. One man and one tank cannot defeat an army. But this army is already defeated. Two weeks, at most, of rations and supplies—that's all we have left, Professor. We cannot attack, and we cannot retreat. But I think Butcher Boy might give command the illusion of action, be a distraction they desire. I think they may give me helicopters. I, too, need a distraction, you see."

"The death of one man?"

Yeshev took the cigarette from his mouth and waved it at his operations officer. "No, Major; nothing so simple as that. If they give me the helicopters, I want Butcher Boy taken alive. And tell Gerisimov I want specifics on the fate of the German spongers—did he or did he not destroy them?"

"Anything else?" said Minski.

"Not until we hear from command, Professor," said Yeshev. "Come, let us look at the map."

Tag wasn't having much luck with Plan B. In the past half hour Fruits had picked up nothing on the ADF bigger than a hog snuffling for acorns, and Tag felt like a blind pig trying to find one. His search-and-destroy orders were moot now; he had Ivan looking for him, but nothing was new in that. Still, Tag couldn't believe that SACEUR's orders had anticipated a massed battalion for him to deal with.

Tag started over again. The immediate objective was to move the Soviet armor out of the village, off the crest of the Jura, where they might try to estab-

lish a corridor back to the east or wheel westward
to lead an assault on the French flank. But he had
to lure them, and that was the rub. Ivan had no air
support, either, and apparently no aerial intelligence,
so Tag would have to keep them close enough not
to break contact but distant enough that he couldn't
be outflanked. In more open country, it would have
been as simple as Apaches leading the cavalry into
a box canyon. But here in the headwaters of the
Danube, in the hills and old forests, it was a tough nut.

Fruits Tutti's voice broke Tag out of his cogita-
tions. "Hey, Captain Max," the loader said, complaint
hovering in his tone, "we gonna set up house here, or
what?"

Porno growled at Tag.

"Naw," said Tag, suddenly realizing what he had
to do, "we'd have to fence it and dig a well."

He cued the radio link in his CVC and said, "Dis-
ciples, this is Butcher Boy. Guide on me."

When the two Bradleys appeared on the crest, Tag
had already reversed the XM-F4 in its tracks. Moving
at a fast walking pace, he led the raiders back up their
trail for more than a mile, then began tacking westward through open forest and rocky, alpine meadows
turned golden in November. The several kilometers of
mountainside between here and the road the Soviets
had used for their approach on the village sloped
gently up to a shelf of rock that formed a continuous
bluff too steep for vehicles. At its closest point, the
bluff was within two kilometers of the village, and
on the map there was a dotted line that meant an
established trail.

When the LandNav indicator put the bluff trail due
north of the No Slack Too, Tag brought his armor to
a halt in the edge of an overgrown orchard, its floor

rust-brown in fallen leaves and apples. Tag opened his hatch and smelled them, their odor reminding him of syrupy homemade wine.

"Fruits," he said, "get your goddamn dog out before he shits in my tank. Open the hatches and air us out. I'll be right back."

Tag found Prentice sitting on the rim of the hatch beside the Phalanx mount on top of his Bradley.

"Chuck," Tag said, "turn the troops loose and meet me over at the Too; I'm gonna get N. Sain and Krager. And watch out for Tutti's dog. Shoot the sonofabitch, if you just have to."

Tag was back in minutes, spreading a sheet from a computer-generated map on the glacis of the No Slack Too for them all to see.

"We're looking at three steps here, gentlemen," he began. "We've got to recon Ivan's situation, draw him to us, and then do what he doesn't expect. If all this works, we can jerk him around all over the map. If it doesn't, we go to Plan C."

Only N. Sain smiled.

"First," Tag went on, "Chuck, I want you to take Villalobos's squad to the base of the bluff and wait for 'em there while they go up for a look at the village."

"Be glad to go myself," Prentice said.

Tag shook his head. "No, stay with the track, Chuck. If it gets messy, I'd rather have you going in for them than the other way around.

"Gaylord, I want you to go with Dunn's squad in N. Sain's track and survey this little piece of real estate right here." Tag tapped the map with his finger. "I've looked at it on the map and on the satellite pictures, but I need somebody on the ground to be sure."

"What is it we're looking for?" Krager said.

"A way off this slope that will get us down here

in this valley, on that road there that crosses back and forth over that stream. See?"

Krager squinted and leaned closer to the map. "Yeah," he said, "I see it. You can go right down this way here." He drew his finger along a marked firebreak.

"Right," said Tag, "that's the obvious way. But what about here"—he indicated a steep pitch off the back of a kilometer-wide outcrop farther east—"can we get down here? The computer says maybe, but that's not good enough."

Krager stood back and grinned. "I always knew I'd replace one of those things someday."

"Okay," Tag continued, "but your people are the ones that have to move fast, Gaylord. Everything depends on our being able to use that slope. If we can, and let Ivan know that we're headed for the river, he'll take your first route, and we'll be at the bottom to meet him. After that, we'll all be stuck in the valley, and there's no way we'll be caught there. We'll have Ivan off the hill and our choice of fields. First chance we get—about here—we'll double back and regain the high ground. Probably pick up a few cheap shots along the way."

Tag turned from the map so he could look N. Sain in his revolving eyes.

"My Dark Disciple," said Tag, "do you see the beauty?"

"Like the cobras of Kali," N. Sain replied. "They grow until long enough to hang themselves by their necks from the rafters. The perfect gift. The first serpent and the omega, circling itself with its tail."

"I think he digs," Ham Jefferson said from the turret hatch.

Tag gave the Rangers time to eat and piss and

study their maps before the Bradleys rolled away in opposite directions, leaving Tag and his crew to coordinate the operation from the No Slack Too.

Tag's mind was still percolating, as it had since early morning, but now he tried to bring it to a simmer, conserve that energy for what was to come. Even in his most hectic moments today, he had felt a kind of calm, a confidence that despite numbers he held the advantage and would prevail. That calm stayed with him now as he wound down his thoughts. He stood in the hatch and smelled again the smell of fallen apples. Tutti was outside the tank with the dog, trying to put him through a series of commands that even an English-speaking dog would not understand. They seemed to be working.

"Lookit dat, Captain Max," Fruits said. "He knows 'sit.' Sit, Porno. Sit, shithead. Good dog."

"Well, don't get too attached to him, Fruits," Tag said casually. "This is as far as he goes with us."

"Hey," Fruits protested, "whatya got against old Porno. He's a goddamn war refugee, Captain. Ain't ya got no heart?"

Porno rolled over on one haunch and began licking his long, red penis.

"Now *that's* why you like him," Ham said from the turret hatch. "You got penis-lickin' envy, Fruit Loops."

Porno lifted his head to lick Fruits's hand. Fruits jerked it away and said, "He can't help it if he's a dog."

Porno put his head against Fruits's hip and panted in adoration, thumping the ground with his tail.

"Tell you what, Fruits," Tag said. "You convince Mr. Jefferson to let ol' Hard-on there ride in the turret, and he can come along. Otherwise, no dice."

"Hell," Ham said, "he smells better'n you do, Fruit Stand. Bring the sucker on."

"Dere, now, Captain," Fruits said. "Don't ya feel better for doin' dat?"

Tag did, and a little silly, but he didn't have long to think about either. Prentice's voice came over the receiver in Tag's CVC: "One-one. One-one." They had reached the base of the bluff. Five minutes later it came back: "One-two. One-two." The Rangers were over the edge and on their own.

Using the LandNav's new wrinkles, Tag began plotting indirect fire on the village, to cover the Rangers' withdrawal if they were spotted. He hated to commit the War Clubs to this, but they were the only effective means he had of laying down several rounds at once, a salvo that would cover nearly two hundred meters of the village perimeter. And he wasn't likely to need them for air defense.

The shadow of the mountain had crept across the meadow when N. Sain and Krager finally returned with good news and bad news.

"The good news is," Krager said, "that we can manage the slope. The bad news is that it's a goddamn thicket. A rabbit couldn't get through there, Max."

Tag nodded and sucked his cheek. "If it's *just* thicket," he said, "it might work in our favor, give us an extra brake on the slope. But if there's any timber, rock slides, anything else in there, we could be in the shit."

"Like I said, Max: good news, bad news."

"Well," Tag said, "there's nothing like that on the real-time pictures. Let's count on it."

Two hours after dark, Tag called in Prentice and Villalobos's squad, and an hour later they pulled into the orchard. Tag was waiting outside when the

Bradley's troop ramp fell open.

"What's the word, Wolfman?" he said to Villalobos.

"They've dug in, sir," Villalobos said, "but it doesn't look like they're making plans to stay."

"Want a beer?"

"Yes, sir."

"Come on over, then," said Tag. "I'll get you one, and you can give me the details. Chuck," he called through the milling Rangers to Prentice, who was just climbing from the cab of the Bradley, "send a couple of men over to draw beer rations. I've got a couple of cases stashed in the Too."

Tag quizzed Villalobos through two beers, getting a fairly accurate picture of Ivan's casualties and the damage to the Soviet armor. From the descriptions, Tag agreed that the hasty fighting positions and lack of movement usually associated with setting up a permanent base indicated Ivan was just in for the night.

"Only thing was," Villalobos added, "there was this one work party out, Captain. They were clearing a vacant lot behind where this one building used to be."

"What were they doing with the rubble?" Tag asked.

"That's just it, sir." Villalobos took a slow drink of his beer. "They weren't doing nothin' with it, just pilin' it up at the side."

"Well," Tag said, "thanks, Wolfman. You've done good. Go ahead and grab some rack."

Before he turned in himself, Tag had a last word with Prentice and Krager.

"What I'm planning," he said, "is this: at about zero-five-hundred hours, I'm going to put a couple of War Clubs into Ivan's position. He'll do a crater rep and find out where they came from. By then, we give him a couple more, and he sees we're moving toward that spine down into the valley. That's when Ivan makes his move, and that's when we get the real-time pictures from the Early Bird. We'll see every move he makes, and he'll think he's got us nailed."

The sentries at their posts that night did not hear the sound blasted down into the buffering trees by the two Mi-28 Havoc helicopters traveling treetop high four kilometers to the west.

8

Gerisimov trembled with excitement and anxiety. The two Havocs sitting on the makeshift landing pad were like gods, deliverance from a bad dream. Their matte-finish skins and dull belly armor looked like living flesh in the weak, milky light of the moon, the noses of the rockets in their weapon pods on the ends of the stubby wings like talons. These were his eyes and his arm, the vision and strength he needed to dismember this Butcher Boy.

But the note from Yeshev that one of the pilots had given him kept Gerisimov only too aware of cold reality. These were no common helicopters. They were two of the squadron attached to command, commonly known to be held there to evacuate the general and his staff. They had never been under fire and looked as sleek and lethal as those that overflew Red Square last May Day. They were only to help him in taking Butcher Boy alive, not to be wasted. In fact, as Gerisimov interpreted the orders in the note, the Havocs were to be protected from all hazard, and he would be held individually responsible for their safe return, as well as for the neutralizing of Butcher Boy. Otherwise, he was to do with them what the situation demanded.

As Yeshev's note concluded, "You now have what you asked for, now do what you say."

Gerisimov was only too aware of how the revolver was passed in this game. It was all win or lose. He would be a Hero of the State or a dead traitor, as command might decree.

Tag awoke refreshed at 0400, and within thirty minutes the Rangers were in the Bradleys and ready to move out. They were to rendezvous with the No Slack Too at Tag's second launch position, and from there the raiders would go into their bait-and-evade maneuver, taking their cues from the real-time images of Ivan's movements that Tag would be collecting from the Early Bird satellite.

Tag programmed one War Club missile for the town center, where he suspected the underground fuel tanks of the village motor pool might remain intact, and the other he targeted for the approximate position of the lot Villalobos had described as being cleared. That done, he made himself a cup of instant coffee with the water Fruits had boiling on a propane ring, ripped open a bag of "Tuna/Noodles," and squatted by the No Slack Too to eat and wait for the Rangers to move into position.

In a minute, Fruits and Ham, accompanied by a slouching Porno, joined him. Tag tossed the soggy leftovers of his MRE on the ground, where the dog wolfed them down with no show of gratitude.

"Dat's right, Captain," Fruits said. "Keep dat up and you'll have a pal in no time."

"Spare me, Fruits," Tag said. "That's the first thing I've seen that that mongrel is good for. What changed your mind about dogs all of a sudden, anyway?"

"Wudn't me, Captain Max; it'z him. Most dogs, dey don't like me. Dis one did. Dat's all."

"Yeah," Ham said, tossing the remains of his meal to Porno, "he thinks you're some long-lost relative."

"Okay," Tag said, rising to his feet, "police the area and saddle up. We've got a wake-up call for Ivan."

Without a command, Porno was up and onto the rear deck of the No Slack Too, where he stood staring expectantly at Fruits, rotating his great loaf of a head from side to side.

"Atta, boy," Fruits said. "See dere; he know the drill already."

There was just a hint of light in the east when Tag gave Ham his order to fire the two War Clubs. The missiles sang from their farings and arced high into the dawn sky. Even before they had reached the apex of their trajectories, Tag had dropped the XM-F4 into gear and was racing to rejoin the Bradleys.

The explosions brought Gerisimov screaming from his shallow sleep, choking on his own voice. Two explosions, two helicopters. The worst possible meaning rose up in the Soviet major's mind. He caught his breath and stumbled from the rubble shelter he had occupied, groping through the darkness in the direction of his tank.

"You," he shouted to the first soldier he saw, "what is it?"

"I . . . I think rockets, Comrade Major."

"What has been hit? Are the Havocs safe?"

"I . . . I do not . . . I'm not sure, sir?"

"Never mind," Gerisimov snapped. "Go."

Gerisimov could see better now. He found his tank and ordered its driver to start the engines, then he set off on foot toward the helicopters. Halfway through the ruins of the village, one of his captains met him.

"Comrade Major," the captain said, "I tried to reach you on the radio, but your driver said you were coming this way."

"Yes, yes," Gerisimov said. "Can you tell me what happened?"

"Two rockets, Comrade Major. No damage. I have my men working on a crater analysis right now."

"And the Havocs, they are safe?"

"Yes, comrade."

"Good," Gerisimov said, relief patent in his voice, "take me to the men who are examining the craters."

The Soviet tankers were very good, and by the time Gerisimov arrived, they had located the launch position of the missiles on the map.

"Well," said Gerisimov, "good work. So, Butcher Boy is still nearby, though not for long, I suspect. Where are those pilots?"

A Ranger rose out of the underbrush and hailed Tag, who stopped the No Slack Too and asked the man where the others were.

"The Bradleys, sir?" the man said. "They're somewhere over there." He waved the muzzle of his M-16 over his shoulder.

Tag found the APCs fifty meters away, concealed in a wild cherry thicket, and called Prentice and N. Sain out at once.

"Listen up," he said. "I've got Fruits patching us in to the Early Bird's signal right now. As soon as he gets a fix, I'll send Ivan a couple more presents, then we'll watch the fun.

"Chuck, go ahead and pull your men in tight. Once we see how Ivan reacts, I want all of you to move into position near our evac route. I'll take the No Slack Too and intercept the bad guys, let them think I'm doing the obvious, then beat it back to you. Got that?"

"Got it," Prentice said, and N. Sain bobbed his head.

Tag found an opening in the trees, from which Fruits could lock on to the satellite and the missiles could be launched, and he brought the No Slack Too to a halt.

"Contact," Fruits Tutti said. "All patched into your screen, Captain Max."

Tag cued up the satellite feed, which threw a fresh frame on his screen about every thirty seconds. He had less than twenty minutes of vision from the fast-tracking satellite, and he hoped it would be enough.

"Fire two, Mr. Jefferson," he said.

Ham tripped the switches and released a pair of War Clubs from the farings. When the missiles passed their halfway point to the target, they were almost directly above the two ground-hugging Mi-28 Havocs, which were en route to the first launch site.

After the third change of frames on Tag's screen, one suddenly showed the white bursts of the War Clubs, followed by shots of men rushing toward the explosions and tanks moving about from their fighting positions. Tag chuckled silently. Ivan was doing his crater rep like a good little soldier, and next he would be coming right into Tag's brier patch.

Tag was so intent on the activity around the dev-
astated village that he paid no attention to the two
anomalous, airborne specks to the east.

The Havocs circled in wide and slow, converging
cautiously on Tag's last-known location, scanning
with their radar and IR sensors for Butcher Boy's
spoor. The heavier belly armor that headquarters had
ordered on these evacuation ships was offset by their
beefed-up microflow turbine engines, but they had
lost some maneuverability, and the pilots had been
briefed on Butcher Boy's effectiveness against aircraft, so they were taking no risks they could avoid.

When the Mi-28s at last hovered over the fermenting
orchard, one of the pilots saw the tread marks that disappeared into the woods beyond, but before he could
draw his wingman's attention to them, Gerisimov's
headquarters was on the radio to report a second
missile attack, this one launched from a point only
minutes west of the first site.

The two Havocs dipped their noses and gathered
speed, beating the tops of the trees with their rotor
blasts.

Tag stood from his screen and leaned out the hatch
to speak to Prentice, Krager, and N. Sain.

"Okay," he said, "it looks like Ivan is assembling
to sweep down the road and cut back east below the
bluff. Let's get in position."

Tag waited until the two Bradleys were loaded and
out of sight before he spun the No Slack Too and
accelerated away at a diverging angle. He wanted
to make contact with the Soviet unit well before it
reached the obvious point for an armored withdrawal

off the mountain, and even farther from the raiders'
actual exfiltration route. But he needed to be in a
fixed position for Fruits to continue feeding him data
from the satellite. Speed was his greatest advantage,
and Tag thought, as he pushed the No Slack Too
through the slalom of timber, *O speed, don't fail
me now.*

A kilometer from the second reported launch site,
the two Mi-28s banked to either side and gained
altitude to scan with their forward-looking sensors in
the forest and thickets below. The pilot who broke
left hung on the air and turned the nose of his craft
to left and right. Two faint heat blips were moving off the edge of his screen. Locking on the azi-
muth, he radioed the other Havoc. The two helicopters regrouped, dropped altitude, and executed a broad
loop that would bring them back on the path of the
heat readings.

The machines stopped, one hovering while the other rose and scanned ahead. There they were, confirmed now: two images moving, less than a kilometer
away. The chopper dropped fast back below the sight
horizon.

Gerisimov's heart raced as he found the map coordinates radioed to him by the Havocs. Butcher Boy
was taking a bad course for the exit into the valley.
It concerned Gerisimov that the pilots had both confirmed only two targets—how he wished he could
order them to attack—but the Americans had given
him an opportunity, by taking the slower route, and
Gerisimov calculated that his own speedy 2S9s could
intercept them. He ordered a formation of seven of the
compact tanks to move out at fastest possible speed

and instructed the Havocs to shadow their targets and keep him informed of their movements. With his superior numbers, he might actually be able to trap Butcher Boy against the falling slope and force a surrender.

Mad Dog drove and pale Rabies sat in the commander's spot, while N. Sain commanded his Bradley from a crouched position like a ball-turret gunner's, in a seat below the Phalanx mount that he personally operated. It lacked the theatrical range of the 75mm rapid-fire cannon on his first Bradley, with its white-phosphorous bouquets—memento mori blossoms—and black blasts of high explosive, its beehive rounds with their thousand tiny scythes reaping death's harvest, but the Phalanx had an authority almost contemptuous of defenses. N. Sain sensed an insolence in its jackhammer brevity, a lethal confidence. And by feeding all of the Bradley's defensive systems through the closed-loop radar on his weapon, N. Sain could also produce shifting, multiple psychedelic images on his console screen, like looking at the world in the fourth dimension, he thought.

He flicked his tongue and programmed the entire array of sensors to track his optical scope 360 degrees as he followed Prentice's APC across a narrow meadow, where he had enough horizon to cast a tracery of limbs and leaves on his screen and record them on tape he would someday edit into his documentary on the victory of death's domain.

Less than halfway through the circuit, as N. Sain squinted into the eyepieces of his optical scope, something at the very edge of the horizon moved in a way it shouldn't, up and down. Yellow air-alert lights

flashed on the console, but the lock was not confirmed, and the klaxon did not sound. N. Sain inter-
rupted the scan and ran back the recording tape.

There. He located the half second of tape, froze
it, and stripped away all but the radar and visual
images. When the program brought these two into
register, there was no mistaking the blur of rotors or
the line of fuselage.

N. Sain turned the sensors all on and set the 37mm
Phalanx to auto-response.

"Sidemen," he said into the pencil mike inside his
CVC, "we have a dark angel over our shoulder, a coy
priestess of Kali, not witness of the blood." He keyed
the TacNet and said, "Listen to the dark disciple.
There is death hovering in the air behind us. We are
not alone."

Tag received the message as he was swinging
the No Slack Too through the meanders of a timber trace. If N. Sain wasn't hallucinating, it meant
Ivan had brought in helicopters. But they hadn't
attacked. Slicks? Observation choppers? Maybe they
hadn't spotted the others yet. Maybe Barlow had
changed his mind. Maybe there wasn't a lot Tag
could do about it right now. He had one shit pot
of bogeys to deal with on his own—known bogeys.
N. Sain and Prentice were going to have to do what
they could.

Prentice activated the air-defense systems in his
Bradley and spoke over his shoulder to the young
sergeant manning the Phalanx console. "Beecher," he
said, "tell the first soldier to have the men break out
the Stingers and be ready to off-load at my command.
We may have something flying."

• • •

The Soviet pilot licked his lips inside his face mask. The moment his radar sensors had detected a beam on his ship, he had dropped below it, not in the radiation for more than a fraction of a second. Too little time, he told himself, to have been detected. Still, he thought it wise to execute a slow enveloping move across the enemy's back path before taking another reading on the targets.

Tag skidded the XM-F4 on locked tracks, released one, braked again, and brought the tank to rest in the margin of a thicket choked with saplings and briers.

"Fruits," he said, "get me locked back on the bird ASAP.

"Ham, shut down everything except your passive radar. N. Sain thinks he saw a chopper."

The gunner shook his head as he reset the defense systems. "No tellin' what that boy might be seein', boss. Just depends on what he's been smokin'."

"Gotcha a feed, Captain Max," said Fruits.

Tag dropped the VLD into place and filled it with the current photograph being relayed by the satellite. He could see the last of the Soviet column leaving the road and entering the woods, but the trees blocked his view of the seven 2S9s that were racing toward his exit route, to intercept Prentice and N. Sain. He examined the picture in the area of the Bradleys' line of march and was about to scan it with an electronic template, used to pick out aircraft images in cluttered or fuzzy backgrounds, when he saw the symmetrical blurs caused by the Havocs' rotors and, on a closer look, the elongated shadows of their bodies beneath.

"Okay, babycakes," he said to Fruits and Ham, "looks like our resident Loony Tune was right again.

There's a couple of choppers shadowing N. Sain and
Prentice, so we're gonna step up the pace. Ham, sabot
in the main tube. Fruits—Phalanx, and be ready to
cover our ass. We're gonna get close enough to give
'em a good sniff."

Tag activated the audio-directional scanner, dropped the No Slack Too into gear, and sped back into
the trees, angling for the Soviet line of advance.

Three kilometers to the north, seven antitank 2S9s
wheeled right and began their envelopment on the two
targets identified by the Havocs.

"Disciple, this is Lazarus. Over."

Prentice paused to see whether N. Sain would
respond, then keyed the TacNet again and continued.

"Disciple, position yourself at point x-ray," he said,
indicating the jumping-off point for their withdrawal.
"I will take security at approaches yankee and zulu.
Over."

Again, there was no response, and Prentice said,
"Lazarus out."

Prentice directed his APC to a fighting position in
the open woods about midway between the alternative
routes Tag would have to the rendezvous. He called
Villalobos to him at once.

"Wolfman," he said, "issue Stingers and LAWs,
but keep the flanks short. We may have to saddle up
and go in a hurry."

"I hear that, Lieutenant," said Villalobos. He turned
away and began bawling orders to the Rangers.

The growl of approaching armor was like the sound
of surf coming through Tag's CVC. He was less than

a thousand meters now from the van of the Soviet column, and he needed a place where he could take them.

"See anything out there that you like, Ham?"

Ham Jefferson had the greatest affinity for ambush and ambush sites of any man Tag had known.

Ham twisted the focus on his scope and said, "I'm partial to this low place, behind that deadfall, just up ahead. Gives us an open back path and cover up to the treads."

Tag silently agreed and put the No Slack Too into the spot.

"Okay," Tag said, "shoot 'em when you see 'em, but keep your lap straps buckled. This is strictly shoot and scoot."

Tag felt the hum of hydraulics as Ham cued to the ADF and brought the turret to bear on its strongest signal. Tag monitored the electronic ears and located a second signal continuing to move east, beyond his position—of course: they were trying to hammer-and-anvil Prentice and N. Sain. The helicopters must have seen them.

"Target!" Ham's voice was still in Tag's ears when the 120mm slammed back in its carriage and the Phalanx lashed out a stream of 37mm depleted-uranium slugs, raking the first rank of Soviet tanks advancing in echelon through the open forest. The sabot from the main tube seemed to be swallowed by the armor of the lead T-80, which rolled another twenty meters before an incendiary plasma of fuel and air belched through the bottom and out the back, kicking up the rear of the tank and enveloping it in flame. The stream of fire from the Phalanx ate into the seam between turret and body of another tank, jamming its machinery, and knocked the track from the drive cogs of a third.

Tag jerked the thirty-ton tank through a standing bootlegger's turn and opened the throttles. The engagement had lasted five seconds.

Gerisimov, riding in the open hatch of his T-80B, was two hundred meters from the ambush, too far for any clear line of sight through the trees, when he heard the guns of the No Slack Too and, moments later, saw the penumbra of the exploding T-80 etch shadows on the trees.

At once, it all became clear to Major Gerisimov. The Havocs had been trailing the two Bradleys; this was Butcher Boy. Alone. There was yet time to call back the tanks he had sent to reinforce the advance party of 2S9s. The smaller tanks could easily engage the Bradleys alone, and he could have Butcher Boy pinned against the falling slope—alive.

Immediately, Gerisimov ordered his main body to form skirmishers—a line that would extend across three hundred meters of forest—and advance at greatest possible speed. Their standing orders since mounting the move against Butcher Boy were to shoot to disable the tank, and to do what they must with the lighter armor. As he waited for the flanks to form, Gerisimov radioed the reinforcements and ordered them to circle back, likewise forming a line. Then, he contacted the Havocs again for an update on the Bradleys' position.

N. Sain had backed his Bradley deep into the briers and brush covering the evacuation slope, crushing a path in which to gather speed when they withdrew, and was pulling back into position at the edge of the thicket, when the air-alarm klaxon blared and the Phalanx snapped into firing position. N. Sain did not take time to confirm the target but released the gun system to full robotic response, bracing himself against the rolling recoil of the Gatling-barreled 37mm. The Phalanx fired one brief burst and fell silent.

At first, the Soviet pilot did not know what had hit him or that he had been hit. As he was dropping back below the radar horizon, after getting a heat fix on one of the now-stationary targets, he felt the Mi-28 shudder against his stick, then saw a geyser of blood and glass showering before him from the impact of a depleted-uranium round with the systems chief in the cockpit just forward of and below his own. Instinctively, the pilot banked in his descent, and the shower of red flesh slapped across the left quarter of his glass canopy. The glancing rounds that struck his reinforced belly armor did not penetrate it, but one had passed through the skin just above the armor seam on the nose, carrying the systems chief's console into his chest and bursting the man like a squeezed grape.

Overrides and redundant systems kicked in automatically. The pilot was another full minute before he realized what had happened and radioed the commander in the other Havoc.

"Disciple, this is Lazarus. What is your target? Over." Prentice felt the sweat running down his palm as he released the key on his radio.

"We have touched the shy, dark angel," N. Sain replied.

"All units, all units, this is Butcher Boy," Tag's voice cut in. "You have bogeys moving on your position."

The transmission ended without a sign-off.

●   ●   ●

Tag was thinking about the armor moving past his flank just before the ambush, thinking there was nothing he could do to help N. Sain and Prentice except tell them it was coming and pray again for speed.

When the flight commander of the Havocs received his wingman's report a surge of combativeness swarmed all over his discipline. His orders were not to fire unless fired upon, and they had been fired upon. Ignoring those orders that enjoined him to protect his aircraft, in favor of those that gave him writ to fire, he pushed his throttles forward, rushing toward the Bradleys' positions, barely twenty feet above the tallest trees.

N. Sain heard Tag's message and quickly moved his APC forward to reinforce Prentice's position. He was no more than a dozen meters into the shadows of the trees when the Mi-28 leapt up out of the trees to the east and raked the head of the thicket with cannon fire, before lumbering into a turn that took it out of sight. The next moment, from in the distance there came the blasts of LAW impacts and the roar of 120mm multiguns from the company of 2S9s, both blotting out the heavy trill of Prentice's Phalanx.

The formation of 2S9s was in a staggered column and driving hard when the first Rangers heard them and alerted the others. And as the first pair of compact tanks came into range, approaching along one of the lines Tag had been expected to take, Prentice's men unleashed a lethal barrage of rockets, supported by the Bradley's Phalanx. Almost at once, the trailing 2S9s returned fire with machine guns and cannons as they broke out of column and scattered for the concealment of the forest.

Commanding from the Bradley, Prentice ordered the squad split into four tank-killer teams to stalk the Soviet attackers.

Four hundred meters from Prentice's position, N. Sain off-loaded Krager and the Rangers and backed his Bradley into the open between the thickety slope and the trees.

Come, lovely one, he thought. *Come, my coy devotee. This is where your heart belongs; this is where you end your day.*

Like a quarterback feeling pressure in the pocket, Tag sensed the tanks falling on his flank before any of his electronics. When the ultrasensitive systems that Fruits had hacked into the Phalanx sensors detected the heat and motion of the Soviets and whirred to lock on target, Tag felt for a moment that it was at his command. But he as quickly realized that, in this context, his robotics had an edge. He engaged them and concentrated on his driving.

The Phalanx cupola spun, locking on targets that appeared for only fractions of a second, firing, and fixing on another, setting up a rhythm of recoil methodical as an assembly line, while the Soviet gunners whistled wild rounds at the wraithlike XM-F4, blinding themselves with the smoke of their own projectiles exploding against tree trunks, filling the air with lost, angry shrapnel.

The Mi-28 came from out of nowhere, strafing blindly as it swept over the edge of the woods. Seeing the Bradley in the open, the flight commander heeled

about and armed his rocket pods. Suddenly he saw
fire spout from the miniature turret on the American
APC and felt the impacts of the Phalanx on the belly
of his ship. The nose dropped; the controls went
heavy in his hands; the tail overrotated, and he was
spinning, out of control. Falling.

Villalobos took one of the tank-killer teams himself, leading the four men in a sprint through the
woods toward the right of the Soviet line of approach,
in the direction of a 2S9 he had tracked when the
formation scattered. The men struggled with their
loads of light antitank weapons that they carried at
sling, ducking to avoid slapping limbs, pounding out
the distance.

Tag steered half blinded by the smoke from Soviet
shells, feeling himself work in rhythm to the thick
stutter of the Phalanx. Later he was to wonder whether it was the smoke or the hypnotic cadence of the
gun that caused him to miss seeing the 2S9 until it
was too late to keep from hitting it.

Picking his way through the timber like a runner
picking up blockers, Tag was too aware of the threat
on his left. He brought the turbines to a scream down
two short corridors in the trees, juked left and right
through thick timber, then broke over the lip of a
dry watercourse and, traveling at forty kph, hit the
stationary 2S9 squarely in the six with thirty tons of
space-age armor.

The slim leading edge of the No Slack Too's glacis collapsed the smaller tank's light rear armor in a
crease across the engine, driving the rear down and
forward, battering the unprepared men inside into
unconsciousness. The No Slack Too rebounded from

the collision and, before Tag could cut the throttle, tried to climb the back of the disabled 2S9. He braked one track and eased the fuel, and the XM-F4 slithered over to one side, coming off the other tank with a hard drop and a screech of metal on metal.

Tag trained the Phalanx on the immobile 2S9, giving himself some distance before taking a shot, but not before four Rangers sprang into the field of his scope, one coming toward the No Slack Too, waving his hands as he ran, and the other three dropping into firing positions with LAWs on their shoulders less than fifty meters away.

Tag turned his tank to face the threat from the flank and threw back his hatch, immediately recognizing Villalobos.

"What's the skinny, Wolfman?" he said as he stood up.

The Ranger slid to a stop and shouted back, "We got four or five of those little tanks scattered, and I think the other Bradley shot a chopper."

"Okay," Tag said, "we'll dust this sucker"—he pointed to the 2S9—"and you people fan out. I got about a dozen on my six."

The Ranger's eyes widened as he whirled and ran back to his team.

"Fruits," Tag said, "pick the grapes."

Fruits, already with the compact tank in his sights, tripped the Phalanx trigger, and the 2S9 ignited like a welder's torch.

Porno cowered in the rear well of the turret, working his lower jaw and emitting a low yowl.

9

Colonel Barlow was not pleased. He too had been monitoring the satellite pictures, and he saw the battle under way, as well as the Jagd Kommandos withdrawing back along the crest of the mountain chain. But he would not break radio silence yet, not until the Kommandos crossed back through the dead zone. Perhaps by then, the war would be over. He looked at his watch.

Villalobos and the men of his tank-killer team knew the seriousness of the situation without having to be told the details, and Tag's wheeling maneuver into a fighting position that covered his rear told them that they had more than a little to do.

The first of the flanking T-80s reared into view over a fallen tree, exposing its thin belly armor, and that was when the first Ranger fired his LAW. The 2.75-inch rocket was next to useless against the tank's armor on the nose and turret, but this was a gift. The rocket ripped through the floorboards of the crew compartment like a shotgun blast, flaying the commander and driver to bloody shreds and wounding the other two men in the turret.

With the sound of the explosion, the rest of the team rushed forward into the woods to meet the advancing tanks that had slowed their attack and begun to scatter, now that one of their number was hit.

The Rangers knew their advantages in this kind of fight, and they knew how to use them. They listened, located their targets, and moved on them, usually from the rear, and always aware that there were more behind. Villalobos motioned his team to string themselves out in the woods roughly parallel to the flanking force, then to move on opportunity. He himself was already advancing on the sound of an engine.

Villalobos smelled the exhaust of the T-80 well before he saw it. He circled to his right, moving swiftly from tree to tree, closing in. Then he caught a glimpse of movement and started forward. In another fifty meters he could see the Soviet tank and its companion 2S9, moving parallel to it on Villalobos's right. The Ranger had only two LAWs remaining, and he knew he needed to make them count. He tailed the tanks for another half minute, until there was enough timber between them to cover his movement.

He dropped to one knee behind the trunk of a larch, extended the tube of one LAW, primed it, and flipped the sight into position. He drew a breath, released some of it, let the sight settle at the fifty-meter mark on the rear grille of the T-80, and mashed the trigger bar. With the multiple internal explosions in the

engine compartment of the tank as a backdrop, he
snatched up his second LAW and raced toward the
position of the 2S9. The smaller tank was making a
twisting turn through the trees when Villalobos saw
it. He took the first cover he could find, behind a rot-
ting stump, and unlimbered his other rocket launcher,
waiting for the target to clear the trees. When the
sound of its motor told him the 2S9 was moving
slowly forward, in his direction, Villalobos peered
around the stump, brought the tube to his shoulder,
and planted a perfect hit broadside, just below the
turret, rocking the compact tank up on its far track.

Villalobos listened a moment after the sound shadow passed, heard the sounds of explosions and machine guns coming from the direction he had sent his
men, and he was off and running again.

The pilot of the remaining Havoc saw, through the
film of blood, soft tissue, and uniform fragments that
had been his systems chief and now was smeared over
one quarter of his cockpit cover, what happened to his
flight commander, saw the wisp of smoke from the
turbine vent, saw the wild auto-rotation of the ship
and the mushroom cloud that rose above the forest
where it crashed. Sobs caught in his chest. It was
all over for him now, his entire career. There was no
surviving this. He opened the throttles on his turbines
and began an ascent.

When reports of two more hits on 2S9s came in,
Prentice ordered the Rangers to advance and moved
his Bradley forward in support, radioing N. Sain to
advise him of the move. He got no response to his
message. Minutes later he was exchanging fire with
one of the 2S9s that was trying to rejoin the main

body, and he hit it with a clean burst from his Phalanx less than one hundred meters from where Villalobos and his men, their LAWs now all expended, were closing in on a lone T-80, each man armed with nothing more than a hand grenade and an attitude.

Tag had several fields of fire on the advancing main body of Gerisimov's battalion, and it did not take him long to employ them all. The lead Soviet elements were on him in minutes, crashing through the woods in what they thought hot pursuit, only to meet hot lead and steel and explosive warheads. Ham had his first target marked before it broke into the open and split the glacis of the tank with a sabot when it did. As the loading carousel spun another round behind the breech, the Phalanx robotics stirred and skeins of depleted uranium swarmed from the barrels of the gun, ripping large trees in half and punching through Communist armor. A T-80 came into the field of fire to Tag's left at one hundred meters, firing on the run. Tag released one of his four remaining War Clubs, which tore the turret back from the body of the T-80 like the top off a cereal box. Ham fired again, crippling another tank and setting it afire. The Phalanx kept up its steady, syncopated tattoo.

A memory flashed through Tag's mind of hunting dove around a water hole at evening, how there were so many in the sky it was hard to pick a target. But the dove weren't shooting back.

Krager was hurrying his men to reassemble and get back in the APC when one of them saw the Mi-28 leap against the sky, saw the smoke as it released a pair of missiles from its weapons pods.

"Incoming!"

The Rangers leapt for cover, and the Phalanx on
N. Sain's Bradley whipped its snout around. The
hastily fired Tree Toad missiles bracketed the APC
and nicked a half-dozen men with flying rocks. Out of
the smoke came the trip-hammer report of the 37mm
and the whistling shape of a Stinger launched from
Krager's shoulder. As the slugs from the maxi-gun
tore through the belly armor of the Havoc, the Stinger
homed on the heat from the nearest weapons pod,
striking the remaining missiles there and blossoming
with them in a consuming cloud of death that rained
twisted, smoking remains of the Mi-28.

Rangers brought Prentice the word that the tanks
to their immediate front were falling back, and they
pinpointed Tag's location as squarely on the far left
flank of their line, where Prentice could still hear
the boom of the 120mm and the beat of the Phalanx.

"Butcher Boy, Butcher Boy, this is Lazarus. Roll to
your right—I say again, your right. Proceed along line
yankee—I say again, line yankee. You're covered.
Over."

"Roger, Lazarus," Tag replied. Then, to his men,
he said, "Keep pouring it on, and hold on to your
hats."

Tag tore ditches with his tracks as he turned the
No Slack Too and ran back hard to the north, quickly
losing contact with the dwindling Soviet assault.

Gerisimov's heart was racing again, and now not
with anticipation of success. Both Havocs lost! But
he had not ordered it. How lame the excuse sounded,
even in his own ears. He was losing armor on every

hand, blocked by infantry in his attempt to encircle
Butcher Boy. Infantry! He ordered his commanders
to cease their advance and regroup. He would not,
whatever else might befall him, he would not be
picked apart one by one. As the stragglers fell back
into the skirmish line, he ordered the tanks of his
headquarters company to close on him and advance.

N. Sain went for the last sounds of the guns and
before he had covered five hundred meters of forest
saw the wedge of main battle tanks as they overran
Tag's last position and continued driving straight for
him.

"Let's play the chorus like we planned it," he said
to MD, and the Rastafarian drummer jockeyed the
Bradley in a kinky turn through the timber. He sped
back down-slope and hit the getaway thicket with
the turbines at high whine, disappearing over the lip
and into the thick briers like a rhino losing itself in
the bush.

Villalobos and the last of his squad had just returned
to Prentice's Bradley when the No Slack Too came
tearing through the trees. Tag identified the APC on
his scope and hit the TacNet.

"Lazarus, this is Butcher Boy. Thanks for the invi-
tation. Can you follow? Over."

"Roger, Butcher Boy. All accounted for. Let's
move. Over."

"Roger. Butcher Boy out."

No longer certain of the disposition of the field,
Tag held as straight and as fast as he could through
the woods for more than a kilometer, then began
to bend back to the west, without slackening his
speed. He was within minutes of having regained the

north-south road when he realized that N. Sain was missing. Apprehensive that radio transmissions might be intercepted, he stopped and called out Prentice for a confab.

"I don't know," Prentice said. "He had downed one of the choppers, I think, and when we moved out, I thought he was pulling up the rear. You know, Max, we all had a lot on our minds."

Tag waved his hand in dismissal. "No, no, Chuck," he said. "I'm not blaming you. Hell, I can't even be responsible for that maniac. But he had Gaylord with him, and that gives me some hope. Damn. I just have a hunch we're going to want him around, before this is all over. Nothing for it right now, though. Let's move."

"Where to?"

"West. It may not matter now, but I want to stay between Ivan and that French flank, just in case."

Tag went as fast as the Bradley could manage, up the road nearly to the village, then back west on the shell-pocked main blacktop, until he found a wooded ridge parallel to the road, where they could have cover and the high ground. He put the No Slack Too and the Bradley in positions to cover the road, broke out the autumn camouflage nets to match the changing foliage, and called a stand down.

The Rangers who piled out of the Bradley were exhausted by their own adrenaline and would have elected Tag dictator of the universe when he produced two cases of beer from his stash in the No Slack Too. Popping open cans for himself and Prentice, Tag ambled over to the Bradley and handed one to the lieutenant.

"Here you are, Chuck," said Tag, handing over the beer. "Perfect pub temperature."

Prentice took a sip, made a face, and said, "Warm as toast, you mean."

"Ahh," Tag said, smacking his lips. "Like mother's milk, you barbarian. Listen, Chuck, don't let your people get too laid-back. This is just the break between rounds, okay?"

Prentice nodded. "What's the plan?"

"I'm not sure yet. I can't get shit from Barlow, but I'm going to try one more time. Here in a minute." He took another long pull from his can. "Meanwhile, let me bounce a few things off you."

"Bounce away."

"Okay. One, Ivan is desperate. Unless I miss my guess, there never was going to be any move on the French flank or any attempt to open a corridor down the Jura. Those shitheads did all this just for us—and that's desperate. Two, our attack orders were just to keep Ivan rattled, keep the pressure on, because some goddamn thing is going on way upstairs, and we're part of it. Three, none of that changes a goddamn thing for us right here, right now. How'm I doing so far?"

"Like a paranoid at a roadblock. Go on."

"Yeah? Well, I'm tired of being the mushroom man in this. And I've got a lousy feeling, Chuck, that all we're doing is hand jive for Kettle or the politicians or somebody."

"I thought SACEUR was your buddy."

"He's a general with a war to win, and I'm a captain—a press-ganged captain, don't forget—who's got nothing but orders. No fucking air support, no communication with command, and no goddamn patience."

"You need another beer, Max?" Prentice asked casually.

Tag laughed and said, "Yeah. Yeah, get me one."

When Prentice returned with the beers, Tag was sitting on the ground with his back against the Bradley. "Thanks," he said, taking the can, "sorry if I sounded off, Chuck."

Prentice shrugged. "You needed to blow," he said. "Got any more steam built up?"

"Naw," Tag drawled, pushing himself to his feet, "I'm gonna go get Tutti to try another burp to Barlow. Make that a belch."

Barlow was in a fix. He thought he knew what Tag was thinking, and he couldn't blame him—he might even be right—but SACEUR was fixated on the notion the First Guards might try to break out and deny the negotiators that card at the peace talks. Barlow was probably the only man, and certainly the only colonel, this far forward who knew about the talks or who suspected the crisis brewing inside the Soviet power structure. The Pact armies were falling back all across Germany, and not always in any organized fashion. Only this morning he had heard the BBC news that three hundred tanks and more than a hundred pieces of artillery had been left behind when the Soviet army abandoned the Netherlands. There just wasn't much evidence of a unanimous will to win within the Kremlin.

But his more immediate problems were what to tell Tag and what to do with the Jagd Kommandos, who had just radioed to announce they were across the dead zone and coming in. By the time Giesla and her three-car contingent arrived at the mineworks, Barlow had made up his mind. He told the radio operator to burp a reply informing Tag that his new orders— orders Barlow was issuing on his own authority— were to continue to observe enemy movements and interdict them only to prevent eastward movement along the Jura. He also told the man to try to make contact with one of the special operations teams in the area and have them link up with Tag. Barlow hoped this might make Tag feel a little less in the dark.

As for the Jagd Kommandos . . . well, he'd just have to talk to them.

"Screwed, blued, and tattooed," Tag said. He flopped back in the commander's seat and wadded the message that Fruits had just decoded for him.

"What's up, bossman?" Ham said, leaning over the hatch above Tag's head.

"Message from Barlow, Hambone. He wants us on the *east* side of Ivan, to monitor movement on the crest of the mountains."

Ham shook his head. "That Barlow may be a brother, but he sure as hell don't appreciate what we do for him."

Tag agreed. "What you say. If I had my druthers, I'd run Ivan's ass through the ringer, but look at us. Without N. Sain or Giesla's Kommandos, we don't have the men or the firepower."

"So?"

"So, Barlow also said we might be contacted by a Special Ops team, but nothing about when or why. It may be that they've got more skinny than we do. Otherwise, it may be a long way home, because Ivan is bound to have some sort of security out, patrols, listening posts, you know. And who knows if he's got any more choppers on call. I reckon it would take us twenty-four hours—minimum—to outflank him and get to the other side, and that's if everything falls our way."

* * *

Gerisimov was a knot of emotions, chief among them fear—fear of the known consequences he would face if he went back now, and fear of the unknown whereabouts of Butcher Boy. The American had vanished. One moment there was a battle, and the next moment only air. Both the Havocs lost! A dozen pieces of armor disabled or destroyed, leaving him fewer than thirty effectives and twenty additional men afoot.

Grim determination began to settle over Gerisimov's thoughts. He would reinvest the village, dig in, and put out scouts to locate the American. To hell with taking him alive—what foolishness. There was no going back for Gerisimov now.

Giesla was adamant—she was going back to Tag.

"Colonel," she said firmly to Barlow, "you must override his orders. Otherwise, I will return in violation. There is no longer any reason for my Kommandos to be out of the field, and very many reasons why they should be—a Soviet battalion of reasons, I believe."

"How will you find him?" Barlow asked, knowing already what his answer would be.

Giesla smiled fetchingly. "Colonel, you can do that for me, can you not?"

Barlow was momentarily nonplussed. "G-go draw fuel and ammo, Lieutenant," he stammered. Lord, she was a beautiful woman. "I'll get you the information you need."

"Thank you," Giesla said. She turned to go and Barlow stopped her.

"And, Lieutenant," he said, "be damned careful. I can't tell you any more than this, but the situation right now does not warrant any unnecessary risks. Do you understand?"

Faint hope gleamed in Giesla's eyes. "Yes, sir," she said. "I think I do understand."

Stretched on the ground in a patch of sunlight at the edge of the camouflage netting, Porno rolled his huge mottled-gray head, opened one eye, and showed Tag his teeth.

Fruits, who was squatted tailor-fashion reading the wiring schemata of the Phalanx radar for pleasure, said, "See, Captain Max, he's smilin' atsya. Good dog, Porno."

Porno thumped his tail.

Tag, leaning over the rear deck of the No Slack Too, looked back at the log book he had open there and said, "Yeah, he might eat just one of my balls now."

With that, Porno rolled to his feet, stretched, arching his back like a cat, and walked stiffly toward Tag. He stopped with his nose only inches from Tag's leg and began to sniff, bobbing his head and never looking up.

Tag stood stock-still, his hand on the butt of the 9mm in his shoulder holster, and watched. After a few seconds, Porno walked back to the patch of sun and flopped down. Jeez, Tag thought, I've got to do something about that boy and his goddamn dog. He wondered whether dogs could be psychopathic.

Ham, who was sitting inside the No Slack Too on radio watch, called from the front of the tank, "Hey, boss, got a telegram for you."

Tag walked to the hatch and took the decoded message from his gunner. "Okay," he said as he finished reading, "give 'em our grid."

"Whose frequency is that, anyway?" Ham said.

"Beats me, but the confirmation code checks out. Let's see if there's any response."

Ham coded the information, compressed it through the computer, and burped it out over the radio. In two minutes a burp came back on the same frequency: the Special Ops team was coming in. ETA: five minutes.

Tag shouted to Fruits, "Tutti, you and your puppy go alert the perimeter that we have friendlies coming through." Then he ducked out from under the cammo net and walked quickly across their position to find Prentice.

The six men of the Special Operations Team were hunched beneath their bulging Alice packs like sculptures of Atlas holding up the world. Tag was glad he had a beer to offer them.

The team leader, a ruddy-faced cajun staff sergeant named d'Salassi, leaned against a tree to unsling his pack before he took the beer and eased himself to the ground beside his load. "Thanks, Cap-tain," he said, a note of Arcadia floating in his bayou drawl. "Didn't know you armor boys had a country club out here."

"Every day's a payday, and steak at every meal," Tag said. He hunkered on his heels and cast a thumb over his shoulder at Prentice. "This is Lieutenant Prentice," he said. "He's in command of the Rangers, what we have left of them. I hope you brought us some nice presents."

D'Salassi shrugged. "We got 'bout enough PE in there to lift the siege of Vicksburg," he said. "What you want to do?"

"Depends," Tag said. "You have any orders?"

D'Salassi shook his head as he drank. "We were saddled up for an op on two bridges down toward Tuttlingen when we got word to link up here. Didn't know there was anybody else out here, except for Ivan." He pronounced it Ee-von.

"Well, you can catch your breath," Tag said, "catch some zees, if you want to, or I can give you some maps to look at, if you want 'em. That'll at least give you an idea of how things lay. I'll brief you later, after we get some evening pictures from the Night Owl. Anything else you need—chow, socks, like that?"

"No, sir," d'Salassi said, wadding the beer can inside his fist, "but I will have a look at those maps."

Porno came from out of somewhere and walked over to d'Salassi, holding his head to be scratched. D'Salassi rubbed him behind the ears.

"Part mastiff of somethin', ain't he?" the sergeant said.

"Or something," Tag said.

"Nice dog, though," said d'Salassi. "They're real good with kids, you know."

The rest of the short afternoon passed without incident, and it gave Tag time to rekindle his very personal animosity toward the nearby Soviet armored unit. By the time the evening satellite images were in hand, he was determined not to have to detour around Ivan. These were his mountains.

Huddled with Prentice, Villalobos, and d'Salassi in the back of the Bradley, studying the pictures and the computer estimates of the Soviet dispositions in and around the village, Tag said, "Okay, we've got the ones down here covering the north–south road, and we've got the ones digging in around the village, but that still leaves us six to ten unaccounted for, depending on how many we knocked out in the action this morning."

"On patrol, you think, Cap-tain?" said d'Salassi.

Tag nodded and said, "But where? They've got a lot of woods out there. Maybe somewhere to the east, along that road; maybe below the bluff, thinking we'll try to hit 'em from there again with indirect fire."

"Fuck 'em," Villalobos said. "We hit the headquarters, Captain, and the rest of 'em won't know whether to shit or go blind. You know how these Soviet groups are organized: cut off the head, and the body, he just flops around."

"I hope you're right, Wolfman," Tag said, "because we don't have much choice."

"Now," he continued, "Ivan's perimeter is thinnest here, on the north side. D'Salassi, I need you to get in there and be in position to blow these four emplacements by zero-four-thirty. Can you do it?"

"I may need to borrow a few of your guys to help hump the gear, but, yeah, we can be there."

"Why blow them, Max?" Prentice asked. "Why not take them out with LAWs?"

"I want to be sure they're neutralized, Chuck, because we'll be coming right through there as soon as they go off."

"Cut across the perimeter, you mean?"

"Right. We'll be through and gone before Ivan knows what's happening. Then—and this is the tricky part—we hit the woods and hiako for the high ground on the north side of the road. That'll leave us exposed on the way up, but it'll still be dark, and we'll have surprise working for us."

"The moon'll be down 'bout midnight," d'Salassi said. "We leave then."

"Wolfman," Prentice said, "get six more men to go with him."

"Got the first one right here," said Villalobos.

• • •

Giesla waited until the moon had set before starting back. As promised, Barlow had supplied her with Tag's location and maps and satellite photos to bring her up-to-date on the situation Tag faced. Ignorant of his plans, she wanted to be within striking distance of the village before dawn. After that, she would see.

She allowed Horst to drive and felt chilly sitting inside the unheated gun buggy with nothing to do but think. Between the hints that Barlow had dropped, the news circulating from the BBC broadcasts, and the rumors she had heard among Captain Lawrence's Rangers, the war was over except for the shooting. That prospect made her long to be with Tag, both as a woman and as a soldier. She wanted time with him without the war intruding, but she wanted most to see him safe.

10

The twelve men, each carrying twelve kilos of plastic high-explosive, plus electrical caps and remote detonators, left in the dark of the moon, moving fast and silently along the top of the wooded ridge. Farther down the slope, at the edge of the trees, the No Slack Too and the Bradley ran their turbines at a whisper as they crept toward the village.

The young captain in command of the 2S9 patrol east of the Soviet bivouac was a barbed wad of anxieties. His stomach had soured hours before and now had settled into a hard, steady ache. In the past two days, he had seen tanks on either side of him explode into fiery balls of hell, become burning coffins for the living crews. He had heard the screams of men in flame. He could imagine Butcher Boy behind every rise of ground.

His patrol plan called for the captain to lay an ambush on the road from the east at 0300 and hold it until 0430, and he was looking forward to being out of the moonless forest. He ate the last of the antacid tablets from his aid kit and stood again in his hatch to listen as they moved. He gulped the frosty night air through his mouth; it seemed to ease the pain in his stomach.

D'Salassi brought his team to halt and called over one of his men and Villalobos.

"Villalobos," he said, "take charge. We're going to slip down to the edge of the trees and see what we can see. If we're not back in, say, forty-five minutes, you go on with the mission."

"Good luck," said Villalobos.

D'Salassi and his teammate left their packs and disappeared into the woods. Moving downhill, it took them less than ten minutes to reach the wood line, about five hundred meters from the nearest Soviet fighting position on the perimeter of the razed village. D'Salassi squatted in the fallen leaves, took out his day/night binoculars, and began scanning the open expanse between the woods at the base of the ridge and the perimeter. There were three or four small orchards left tattered by the shellings, some low rock walls around garden plots, much overgrown meadow, its hay not mowed this season, and two natural water courses cutting through all of it.

D'Salassi marked the locations of the three Soviet emplacements that he could see and made a mental map of the terrain, then passed the glasses to his teammate. They were back with the others in less than thirty-five minutes.

D'Salassi huddled with Villalobos under a space blanket, briefing the Ranger on the map by red-filtered flashlight.

"You take half of the men and penetrate the perimeter here, along that creek bed," d'Salassi said, "the others and I'll come in by this other one. Take those two baby tanks, here and here. Once you set your charges, get everyone back in the creek and wait for me to pull the trigger."

"And then?" asked Villalobos.

"And then," d'Salassi said, "keep your eyes open for your ride."

Tag looked at his watch: 0300. Fifteen hundred meters away in the darkness lay the Soviet perimeter. From here, the slope became too steep for the Bradley to quarter across, so their final approach on the village would have to be in the open. Through his infrared scope, Tag could see that the photos and maps were right: it was good country for what they had to do. There was plenty of roll to the land, enough to duck in and out of and make a hard target, but he was counting on the confusion set off by the plastic explosives to help cover the dash, as well. Add to that a few smoke rounds and a screen once they were inside the perimeter, and Tag reckoned his chances better than—well, better than nothing, at least.

Giesla had to clench her teeth to keep from snapping at her driver. Horst's careful navigation through the margins of radioactivity had seemed excruciatingly slow to her, and something about the cold stillness of this moonless night was proving eerily unsettling. She felt silly and melodramatic for believing that things were "too quiet," like the histrionic heroine in a cheap horror film. Still, she had to struggle with herself to keep from ordering Horst to let her into the driver's seat. She wanted things to happen quickly now. She wanted to tell Tag there was no point in risking himself. She wanted an idea to come to her, one that would get her around the Soviet position and to him faster.

The three gun buggies rolled down the road by starlight.

Villalobos crouched behind the corner of a ruined rock wall at the corner of a blasted orchard and took out his day/night binoculars. It was fifty meters through high grass and bushes to the dry creek bed that ran another hundred meters into the village and passed beneath a concrete footbridge that lay between two of the Soviet 2S9 tanks positioned in that quadrant of the perimeter. The water course was rocky, with steep sides overgrown by brush and dead weeds—a good approach.

The Ranger sergeant turned his glasses on the tank positions themselves and scanned for movement. Nothing. Probably asleep, Villalobos thought, except for one on watch inside. Or maybe they're all asleep inside.

He flexed his fingers in the cold and motioned his team to move up. One by one, he sent them crawling through the high grass and into the creek bed. As each man moved out, Villalobos eyed the Soviet positions. When the other five were in the creek, moving toward the cover of the footbridge, he put away the glasses and slid forward under the weight of his pack into the slick, bent grass of the path his men had made and slithered down the bank.

The bottom of the creek bed was made of solid plates of rock, descending in small steps between each one, and the men moved easily forward and into the concealment of the concrete bridge. The darkness there was so deep that Villalobos could not communicate by hand and arm signals but had to cup his hand over each man's ear to give them their instructions. Two men from the Special Ops team slipped silently out of their packs and grounded their rifles. From the packs, each of the two took a .22-caliber semiautomatic pistol and screwed a silencer to its muzzle. They checked their knives and the garrotes in their breast pockets, then tapped Villalobos in the darkness to signal that they were ready.

Intended for bicyclists and pedestrians, the concrete slab of the bridge was wide enough for a car or truck or a 2S9, and it lay to the rear of a line drawn between the two Soviet positions that it connected. When Villalobos returned the men's signal, they stood, reached up, gripped the edge of the slab, and pulled themselves onto it. At once they were moving in opposite directions into the rubble of houses that used to stand along the stream.

D'Salassi felt the ice crusting on the front of his fatigues and hunched his shoulders forward to try to keep the cold off his chest. The water course he had led his team through was a wider, shallower depression than the one Villalobos had come down, and a seeping spring had kept a long stretch of it wet at the bottom. It also brought him much closer to one of his objectives than to the other, with little rubble for cover to the wide side. On the short side, where

a 2S9 had made fighting position from the remains
of a gutted stone storage shed, d'Salassi was close
enough to hear one of the Soviet soldiers pissing on
the ground. He waited until he heard the man finish
and a hatch bump shut and then dispatched two of his
own men to reconnoiter.

The Soviet patrol commander was miserable with
gas. The stomach tablets had killed the acid pain, but
now he could not keep from farting. Standing in the
turret was impossible—he would have been cutting
onions, as his mother used to call it, directly in the
face of his gunner. So the young captain sat on the
cold top of the turret, his legs dangling through the
hatch, and tried to remember how to let the pressure
off a little at a time, the way he used to in lectures at
the officer academy—classroom creepers, they were
called—and he really had been quite clever at keeping
a straight face.

Lost in this protocloacal recollection, the captain
almost missed seeing the three Jagd Kommando
attack vehicles passing through the cocked jaws of
his ambush. A movement at the edge of his vision
momentarily startled him into embarrassment at his
thoughts, then horror that he was wool-gathering at
this moment—a moment when three German spongers
were already nearly out of his kill zone. He ripped a
blaring fart as he hunched forward and into the hatch,
giving his gunner orders to fire before alerting the rest
of the ambush, who, if they had spotted the vehicles,
were awaiting his command.

Giesla thought she saw the break in the trees she
was looking for, one that would give them access
to the ridge north of the village, and she was in the

motion of raising her left hand to signal Horst, her
mouth opening to form words, when the car behind
her, the last of the three, the one crewed by Karl
and Uwe, exploded in an orange ball of fire. The
concussion drove her own car forward, and flying
metal fell like hail on its cowling, missile racks, and
empty recoilless rifle tubes. Mathias Betcher, in the
car ahead of her, bolted forward, and Horst did not
have to be told to follow.

A second high-explosive round whistled into the
macadam where Giesla's car had been a half second
before, and from the right front came a thudding
volley of heavy machine-gun fire that battered the
armored nose of the Kommando vehicle and splintered the fiberglass cowl.

Horst and Giesla left the road, with her steering
from the loader's seat, while he tried to wipe away the
blood that flowed from a gash across his eyebrows.

"Give it gas, Horst," Giesla said. "Do not stop."

She fought the wheel over the shoulder of the road,
sideways down a steep ditch, up the other side with
the engine lugging, and then onto a falling, wooded
slope that seemed to get steeper as it fell.

"Stop, Horst. Brake us," she said.

The gun buggy came to a halt quartering downhill
on a grade Giesla was not certain she could climb. As
she scrambled to get Horst into her seat and herself
behind the wheel, Giesla called up her memory of the
map and remembered the deep, narrow hollows that
clawed the edge of the road here. Some of them fell
almost sheer their last few meters. Above her and to
the right but very close by came the crack and hiss of
an ATGM igniting, followed by the muffled booming
of it exploding inside armor and a racking burst from
the minigun on Betcher's gun buggy.

She pushed up the flap of skin hanging between Horst's eyes, pressed a bandage against it, and put his hand over it.

"Hold that," she said.

She ran around the car, swung into the seat, and keyed the radio transmitter, ordering Betcher to fall back on her.

Tag heard the report of the 2S9's 120mm multigun and saw the flare of the gun buggy engulfed in flame, and as he snapped to his feet for a better view from the hatch, he caught his still-tender shoulder on the rim and winced as the second Soviet shell split the blacktop three kilometers away.

"What's that shit?" Ham Jefferson said through Tag's CVC. "Don't suppose Wolfman overshot his objective, do you?"

Tag shook off his pain and said, "No, Mr. Jefferson. You know those legs aren't gonna walk any farther than they have to. Maybe Ivan's shooting at himself."

Tag thought it was nothing but a good thing that the Soviets were occupied with something on the other side of the perimeter, until minutes later he heard Giesla's call to Betcher on his own TacNet. Tag went tingling numb, as though flash lightning had passed over him, and his mind froze in a single thought: *I've got to get her out.*

But as the wheels of thought thawed again, a devastating reality hit Tag: he could not help her. He had two dozen men, two pieces of armor, and a mission all at risk, and he could not sacrifice them for a suicidal attempt to rush past the Soviet guns and reach her. He looked at his watch: 0350. More than a half hour until he could move, until Wolfman and

d'Salassi blew him a breech in the defenses. And he
had to wait on them.

There was no more firing for the moment from the
distant ambush, and Tag did not tell his men what he
had heard.

Villalobos lay in the creek bed beneath the concrete
footbridge gulping for air. His heart had already been
picking up tempo as he waited for the two Special Ops
assassins to return. He had just flipped back the cover
on his watch to check the time, when the ambush of
the Jagd Kommandos broke on the other side of the
village, and suddenly that racing heart was in his
throat: his first reaction was that it was Tag. But
moments after the last echoes of shots had faded, the
two Special Ops men dropped back beneath the bridge
and reported that there were no men outside the tanks.

After that, Villalobos had only thirty minutes to get
the charges set and no time to think.

Polaris. Big Bear. Little Bear. Ah—Orion, the hunt-
er, a solid band of stars at his waist.

Mmmm.

Some powerful fucking connection there. Celestial
girding above the bowl of the belly, seat of all power,
heap of steaming guts, spurting hormones.

Mmmm.

Only kept in by that divine belt. He-he. Keep it
zipped, Jack. Keep your pants on, pal.

Mmmm.

N. Sain lit his butane lighter and took another long
draw on the stubby pipe that contained shavings from
a dwindling brick of Amsterdam hashish he had been
carrying these past three months, and he gazed again
at the night sky. From somewhere far away, beyond

the valley he had fled to and crossed, beyond the place in the mountains where he had fought the Havocs, beyond the bluff and the woods, he heard the sound of cannon and rocket fire.

He focused his attention on the direction of the sound and relit his pipe. After a few minutes, as his concentration began to wane and he fingered the lump of hash in his pocket, contemplating another hit, he heard Giesla's brief radio transmission and broke into an intense, dreamy grin.

N. Sain put away the pipe, climbed down over the side of the Bradley, and woke Krager, who was wrapped in his sleeping bag on the ground nearby.

The grizzled Ranger came awake at once, and N. Sain said to him, "True believer, blond Kali, consort of the Avatar, she has met the deniers of death, much to her surprise."

Krager tried to translate but ended up saying, "What the hell—"

"Our valkyrie has been fallen on by the bear."

"Lieutenant Ruther? Giesla—ambushed, you mean?"

"We have the sound of the guns," N. Sain said, leaning close enough for Krager to smell the thick odor of cannabis, "let us fly to them."

Christ, Krager thought, *here I am jumping to this hophead's hallucinations*.

"Where?" he said.

"The alpha and omega, the point of eternal return," crooned N. Sain, edging into song. "Show your map to me, and I will show you mine."

Krager rousted Sergeant Dunn, told him to have the men saddle up, then, sighing and wagging his head at himself, shook a map out of the cargo pocket on his leg and climbed into the hatch of the Bradley.

•   •   •

The destruction of the first tank that he ordered forward had shaken the Soviet captain, and it was several minutes before he could regroup himself and his men to press the attack, as Comrade Major Gerisimov had ordered. He knew the lay of the land, and he had seen where the Jagd Kommandos went. The pain in his stomach was gone, forgotten in the activity of battle and its excitement. The captain's mind was alive now, recalling exercises he had been through, lectures he had passed gas through, plotting his tactics to close the net on the German spongers. He fanned out his five surviving tanks and pushed across the road and into the trees.

Gerisimov wasn't budging. He had been lured into Butcher Boy's designs already, and this deception on the road would not work on him this time. He had ordered his captain to continue the pursuit, but he would not commit more units. Not yet. Gerisimov lit a cigarette and saw himself as a scarred and wily veteran.

0410. Villalobos could hear the men inside the 2S9 more clearly than he could his own troops who were planting the charges under it. He shut the cover on his watch softly and continued to scour the darkness for signs of movement, praying no sergeant of the watch or bored duty officer would come out to inspect this arc of the perimeter. His luck held. The two Special Ops men had the 2S9's treads and belly packed with thirty-six kilograms of primed plastic explosive in less than five minutes, and five minutes after that they were all back beneath the bridge.

•   •   •

By moving continuously against the fall of the slope as they tried to put distance between themselves and the road, Giesla and Betcher soon found they had nowhere to go. The spine of ridge above the hollow at last played out and fell nearly sheer to rejoin the rest of the mountain. With her own motor off and the bat-wing door of the crew cowl open, Giesla could hear the formation of toy tanks closing on them.

"Mathias," she said as Betcher bailed out of his own vehicle and ran to join her, "find a place to fight from. We cannot go forward here."

Betcher stopped where he stood and cocked an ear to listen to the sound of approaching tanks.

"*Ja,*" he said, his face grim. "I will take this side." He indicated the side of the ridge nearest his car and turned to rejoin his loader.

Giesla made a quick survey on foot and found a scatter of fallen trees among jumbled boulders on her side of the ridge. She spun her gun buggy into position behind the deadfalls, leapt out to load all six recoilless rifle tubes, then checked again on Horst. He had tied the bandage around his head and stopped the bleeding, but she could see he was still dazed from the wound.

"Horst," she said, "listen to me. Get out and go on from here on foot."

"What?"

"It does not matter where," Giesla continued without pausing. "Just go. Lose yourself in the dark, try to find Max—anything, only go."

"I cannot do that," said Horst. "I will not leave you here alone."

"I am not alone; I have Mathias. And you have an order. Go."

She got Horst out of the seat and pressed an H&K

9mm submachine gun into his hands, along with a pouch containing two more thirty-six-round magazines, then nearly pushed him down in her hurry to get him away from there.

As Horst clattered down the rocky ridge, skidding on his heels, Giesla saw the first shadow of movement in the forest that told her the tanks were closing in.

Tag keyed the TacNet twice to signal d'Salassi and Prentice, then eased the No Slack Too forward out of the timber, gathering speed slowly over the rolling terrain.

Villalobos and the men huddled under the bridge felt the earth shake and the air ripple with the detonation of d'Salassi's charges. Villalobos raised the antenna of his own microwave remote detonator above the banks of the creek bed and pressed its red button.

The almost eighty pounds of explosives under each of the tanks that they had mined went off with such force that the thinly armored 2S9s literally came apart in blazing geysers of ripped and twisted metal. One hissing chunk the size of a motorcycle hammered into the creek only feet from the bridge, creating an explosion of pulverized rock, as hundreds of smaller chunks fell all around. The men were battered by the concussion, nicked by stones, half stunned and half deafened, but Villalobos had them out of the creek and dispersed into firing positions before the smoke from the explosions had quit rising.

Tag opened the throttles and ordered Ham, "Fire smoke."

In rapid succession, two smoke rounds left the 120mm, and Tag said, "Load sabot."

Keeping the XM-F4 between the Bradley and the remainder of the Soviet perimeter, Tag used all the speed that the APC could coax from its turbines, making straight for the first two of the four thunderous explosions that had shattered the perimeter's northern rim.

At the first water course, the shallow depression that d'Salassi and his men had used, Tag triggered his smoke generator, sending billows of concealing white from the rear of the No Slack Too, while d'Salassi and the others clambered in the back of the Bradley. At Villalobos's position, Tag let the Bradley cross the footbridge first, while Ham turned his sights and sensors on the interior of the perimeter.

Because the first reports were so confused, Gerisimov did not know for fully five minutes that an entire sector of his perimeter had been breached. He hurriedly dispatched two of the T-80s he had held in reserve to plug the hole. As they sped across the shattered remains of the village, Gerisimov came to the realization that Butcher Boy had split his command, that the enemy vehicles his patrol was pursuing were not decoys to a trap. He ordered six more tanks from the perimeter to go in support.

"Targets," Ham called. "Two approaching at three o'clock."

"Rip 'em," Tag said, and the 120mm bucked back in its dampers, its whining sabot round splitting the glacis of one T-80 between its hatches, like the grin on a Halloween pumpkin, except the white-hot glow behind the smile was from burning men and fuel, not a single candle.

The second Soviet tank veered right in evasion,

opening its flank to the Phalanx, which shredded the treads and drive carriage and punctured the engine compartment, setting the motor afire.

Tag hit the smoke generator again, dragging a screen of white behind him as he raced to overtake the Bradley that had already cleared the perimeter and was going for all it was worth toward their rendezvous in the hills.

11

Giesla had a target now in her infrared sight, a lone 2S9 sent to investigate this narrow rib of the mountains. The pod of three 106mm recoilless rifles on the left side of her vehicle tracked silently on its electro-hydraulic carriage. The heat sensor in the armored nose had, amazingly, survived the earlier machine-gun fire, and with it Giesla had locked her rack of ATGMs on a second tank waiting farther back, at the head of the hollow. She programmed all four of her missiles for the single target, not trusting to a single shot through all these trees. She fought off a shiver and licked sweat from her lip.

The approaching 2S9 was small enough to follow the same alleys through the trees that the Jagd Kommandos had used, slowly tacking its way toward them, but Giesla could see through her scope that the gun was not in an attack attitude. She would not allow herself to hope that the tank might not find them.

When the 2S9 was seventy-five meters from her, it suddenly stopped and swung its turret to the left, in Betcher's direction. Giesla did not hesitate. She pulled the electronic lanyard on the bank of 106s and sent three rounds of high explosive screaming into the tank. The flaming impact smashed in the entire side of the 2S9 and slammed the small tank against a thick fir tree, where it flared its fuel and set the lower branches of the fir ablaze.

Giesla was reaching for the switch to fire the missiles when a tube-launched Songster missile from a tank farther to her right, one she had not located, ripped into the ridge just in front of her parapet of deadfalls. The explosion lifted logs almost as large as her car, and Giesla felt herself driven backward, the rear tires beginning to lose traction and slide sideways down the hill. She hit the starter and found first gear as more missiles sang through the trees and explosions ripped trunks and limbs all above and around her. Tracers from machine guns stitched the air.

Giesla could not find traction. The lug-studded honeycomb tires on the rear spun, caught, let go, and spun again, as the heavy end of the car twisted down and around. She cut the wheel and let the nose drop until she had executed a 180-degree turn, then hit the gas again and began to move, still spinning tires and losing the fight with gravity on the steep slope of the ridge. Another explosion rocked her already teetering gun buggy as a second Songster tore into the timber behind her. Twice she tried to turn back up the slope, and twice the rear end began to skitter and slide. After the second attempt, she let the gun buggy slide to a stop, braced by a slender oak, grabbed the loaded patrol harness from beneath her seat, took the other MP-5 submachine gun from its rack, and threw back the bat-wing door of the cowl, scrambling out and into the dark of the woods only seconds before another of the 2S9s found the gun buggy in its sights and blasted it to scrap.

Giesla fell into the shadow of a tree created by the explosion and fire. She was safe for the moment, for no vehicle could follow her on this slope, and she quickly slipped into the patrol harness and inventoried her ordnance. In addition to the 9mm Sauer pistol in her shoulder holster, she had four more banana clips for the MP-5 on the harness, as well as a half-dozen grenades and a slim-bladed knife. She adjusted the straps on the harness, took a breath, and began making her way around the point of the ridge, hoping to come back on Betcher's position on the other side.

From his vantage point on the wooded hillside, Tag could cover the entire Soviet formation in the village, although his view of the east–west road and the reinforcing column that Gerisimov had dispatched was blocked. He had to get to Giesla, but he had also to keep Ivan off balance enough to give himself enough time. He began plotting targets among the tank emplacements.

"Targets, Hambone," he said. "Mark four."

"Eeny, meeny, miney, and moe," Ham said. "Marked to spark and bark, bossman."

"Fast as we can, gentlemen," said Tag. "Let's see some shooting."

Two of the targets Tag had designated were on the perimeter nearest the No Slack Too's location, and the other two were in the center of the formation, in what Tag hoped was the headquarters platoon. His crew got off their four shots in less than thirty seconds and totaled four clean hits from twenty-five hundred meters.

Tag took no time to admire the work, however, and was crashing the XM-F4 through the brush toward the top of the hill where Prentice was waiting before the last echo of the gun had died.

Gerisimov's gritty image of himself was shattered, and the cigarette hung dead in his lips. He was oblivious to the sting of the antiseptic that the medic was using to clean his lacerations and shrapnel wounds, oblivious to the cold of the early morning and to the heat from his burning T-80B nearby. He thought with grim humor how silly it was to treat his wounds only so he could be fit for a firing squad.

A lieutenant with a smudged face and torn uniform came running up to Gerisimov and said breathlessly, "Comrade Major, we have lost eight pieces and four entire crews. What are our orders, comrade?"

"Orders?" Gerisimov asked weakly, the cold cigarette dangling from his lower lip. "We are going to destroy Butcher Boy, of course. Load the men. Let those afoot ride on the decks. We're going. We're all going."

To hell, he thought.

N. Sain cut the corner of the intersection of the two main roads outside the village and edged his Bradley along just inside the trees until he had a clear view of the village. He watched the Soviets break bivouac and form up to move, with men swarming over the decks of the tanks for space to ride. As they clattered out of the village on the blacktop, the first gray of dawn was beginning to break in the east.

N. Sain waited until the Soviet column had cleared the far side of the village, then he pulled onto the road himself and shadowed them at long distance, smiling merrily and bobbing his head to the beat of "Ruby Tuesday" being played through his CVC.

One vehicle destroyed and the other pinned down: the once-anxious Soviet captain was beginning to like the prospects of this action, despite the loss of one of his own tanks. But now he could find no good way to advance on the remaining Kommando car without exposing another of his 2S9s to fire. He ordered one man from each crew to fall out with a personal weapon. They were going to take the sponger on foot.

By the time Gerisimov's disoriented formation had regrouped to leave the village, Tag was leading Prentice's Bradley in a headlong dash down the wooded hillside toward the road. The No Slack Too bucked and jolted through rocks and saplings, smashing a path for the loaded APC, heedless of everything except covering the distance to Giesla. Tag brought them across the road seconds before the remains of the main body of the battalion came into view. As he entered the woods, the sounds of cannon fire ceased and a steady racket of heavy machine-gun fire began.

"Lazarus, this is Butcher Boy," Tag radioed to Prentice. "Full antitank deployment. Have the men stand by for action."

"Roger, Butcher Boy."

Within one hundred meters, Tag had a blip on his heat seeker, then several, as the reinforcement of 2S9s closed on the pinned-down Jagd Kommandos along a course converging with Tag's own.

"Lazarus, this is Butcher Boy. Do you have the bogeys at two o'clock? Over."

"Roger, Butcher Boy."

"They're yours, Lazarus."

Tag continued to speed forward, leaving the Bradley behind. After another two minutes, Tag slowed their pace, opened the hatch, and began to listen intently as he crept toward the guns. He thought he could make out three different heavy machine guns firing in rotation and not changing their positions. Got them cornered, for sure, Tag thought.

Out of the darkness, Tag saw a figure emerge— a man waving and calling Tag's name—and Tag recognized the voice of Horst.

He braked the XM-F4 and bounded out of the turret, rushing to help the stumbling Jagd Kommando.

"Horst," Tag said, taking one of the man's arms and throwing it across his shoulders, "where are the others? Lieutenant Ruther—Giesla—is she all right?"

"Trapped, down there," said Horst, twisting against Tag to point toward the sound of the machine guns. "I don't know—one car, our car, destroyed. But Sergeant Betcher is trapped."

"Lieutenant Ruther, though—she was with you, right? Where is she? Is she okay?"

"I—I don't know. She told me to leave. I left. She stayed. I don't know."

"How can we get to her, to them?" Tag said.

"They are sending troops in on foot to overrun them. I saw, back there. They were crawling under the machine guns' fire."

Mathias Betcher had to admit that his situation was not ideal. His vehicle could not move, both because any movement would expose him to enemy fire and because the left-rear tire had been blown to gobbets by a Songster's near miss. As a result, none of his primary weapons—106s, ATGMs, or minigun—could be brought to bear. It was possible to dismount the minigun and relocate it in a bracket on the roll cage, or even to fire it from a tripod, but to do that he would need not to be pinned in his seat by the steering wheel and the collapsed side door. He watched the tracers streak overhead and held a small Walther submachine gun in each hand. He knew what was coming.

In the seat beside him, Jan sat slumped dead, his chest ripped open by shrapnel from the same blast that had crushed Betcher's side of the car.

Tag settled the battle harness straps on his shoulders and jacked a round into the chamber of his CAR-15.

"Now listen up," he said to Ham, who sat with his head out the commander's hatch, "you've got to keep them off me, Hambone. Horst says he counted five tanks, but I've only got three I can hear, so be careful. As soon as you get their attention, I'll snatch the survivors and get back to you."

"Just like that, huh?" Ham said.

"Just do it," Tag said.

Porno, who had been sniffing at the back of the tank after having jumped out through the open commander's hatch, loped into the emerging shadows, moving parallel to Tag's charge through the trees.

The thin carpet of leaves did little to save Giesla's elbows and knees from the rocky rim of the ridge, where she low-crawled to stay as close to the top as she could and still be beneath the strata of raking tracers that snapped the sound barrier only inches above her head. In the rising light, she could make out Betcher's vehicle thrown at a crazy angle behind a rock outcrop, with one door missing and one rear tire in shreds. At first she could not see the figures inside and assumed Betcher and Jan both dead. But then she caught a glimpse of movement and crept forward until she could see that Betcher, at least, was alive. And that was when she saw the first of the men on foot pull himself on his belly up on the outcrop.

Giesla pulled the MP-5 to her shoulder and tried to relax and find her sights in the dim light. The man on the rock rose to a crouch and filled her rear aperture. Giesla fired a five-round burst. The three 9mm slugs that struck the Soviet trooper spun him to his feet and dropped him dead.

Giesla scuttled forward, working toward the top as close as she dared, trying to get a better angle from which to cover Betcher's position. She knew he was alive, but something had to be very wrong for him not to leave the disabled car. If she could not stop them, the men on foot would easily overwhelm her favorite sergeant.

A smattering of fire from men with AK-47s came from behind the outcrop, all of it flying high and wild above Giesla, and the heavy machine guns continued to rake the trees. She burrowed through the leaves drifted against the ground-sweeping skirt of a fir tree and moved into the cover of its trunk.

Ham could see two of the tanks on his screen now and hear the third, and that was good enough, especially with the whomp of detonating LAWs and the hammering of machine guns he could hear behind him as Prentice and his men engaged the reinforcements. Ham locked one of the last two War Clubs on one target and laid the main tube on the other.

"Lord, love an ambush," he muttered and released the War Club. As it cleared its faring, Ham triggered the 120mm, and both of the 2S9s were transformed into burning carcasses.

"Reload, Fruit Loops," Ham said, and he dropped the No Slack Too into gear, following the muzzle of his gun to the Soviet position.

Tag had worked himself close enough to determine what Ivan was shooting at when the No Slack Too struck. The machine guns all fell silent, and he saw a flash of movement in the far woods that he hoped was the third Soviet tank. Keeping one eye cocked in the direction of the movement, he began darting from tree to tree, steadily making his way across the narrow top of the ridge toward Betcher's position on the other side.

Porno skulked along silently far behind him.

Tag saw the first of the men on foot when he was still more than a hundred meters from the beleaguered Jagd Kommandos, and he began working himself into position for a shot. The Soviet soldier was on one knee and calling out orders to the other reluctant troopers who continued to shy from the bursts of 9mm fire that Giesla was pumping from her blind beneath the fir tree. Tag stopped and looked again and now could see the kneeling man was fixing a rifle grenade to the muzzle of his AK.

Tag was in the act of rolling the stock of his CAR-15 to his shoulder, when there was a blur, a low growl, and the heavy sound of colliding flesh off to his left. He dropped to one knee, swinging his rifle for a shot, and saw a tangle of man and dog writhing on the ground.

Porno rolled free, separating the Soviet trooper from his helmet in the process, and when the man started to rise, the big dog was on him again, taking the entire girth of the man's head in his jaws and slinging him savagely. There was a wet, ripping sound, like the pelt peeling off a rabbit, and Porno fell back on his hams, the human scalp hanging from his mouth.

The man rose in pain and horror, and Porno had him by the throat before he could scream, crushing his windpipe with vise-grip strength.

Tag spun back just as the grenade left the other trooper's rifle. Tag shot him, and the grenade detonated somewhere behind the outcrop of rock. One of the two remaining Soviets raised up for a look, and Giesla shot him from behind. The last man dove over the outcrop in desperation, only to be cut down by Betcher's twin Walthers.

Giesla rushed forward, not looking for cover now, and she came within a hair of blasting Tag when he vaulted over the rocks and executed a parachute landing fall almost at her feet.

Their eyes said all that needed be. They touched briefly, and Giesla said, "Help me, Max. Mathias is trapped in the car."

Betcher waved one of his weapons and said, *"Ja,* I am okay. Only get me out and I can fight."

Tag found a tire tool in the possibles box and used it to shatter the steering wheel, setting Betcher free. The Kommando sergeant grunted and pulled himself out of the cockpit. He was obviously in pain, but would only wince with his eyes and say, "I am bulletproof, but too fat, too fat."

"Can you travel?" Tag said. "I've got the No Slack Too and the boys waiting for us."

"Where?" Giesla said.

"Just keep listening," Tag said, "and you'll find them."

"True believer," N. Sain said to Krager over the intercom, "do your followers desire death's dark harvest? Are they ready to consummate the inexorable will of the cosmos and bring our enemies to their perfection? Do your legs want to kick some butt?"

"Say on," Krager replied. "We are of one bloody mind, one deadly heart."

"They flee from us that one time did us seek. Let us jump-fuck their pipes. Do you like taking them from the rear?"

"Yeah," Krager said, grinning despite himself, "it's a truly tantric posture. Can you put me on 'em."

"I am but death's procurer," N. Sain said modestly. "I can do no less."

He waited in the lee of the hill until the last of the Soviets had left the road to move en masse on the scattered raiders of Tag's command, then N. Sain booted his throttles and flew after them, imagining Rangers sown in their ranks like dragon's teeth.

Prentice's Rangers had gotten good at killing Communist tanks in the forests of Germany, and they were proving it again. The action unfolded like ballet in Prentice's mind.

The Rangers in Villalobos's squad lost no time getting out of the Bradley and moving out fast parallel to the approaching Soviet column. When the lead tank fell into Prentice's sights, he ordered Beecher to trigger the Phalanx. The depleted-uranium slugs blew plugs of armor through the interior of the

2S9, which shuddered and stalled under the jet of fire, before bursting into flame.

Without its load of men, the Bradley was uncommonly agile and fast under Prentice's touch at the controls. As he pulled back to his secondary position and the Soviet formation came on-line, the Rangers fell on the maneuvering tanks from the rear, often launching their LAW rockets from fifty meters or less into the sheet-metal armor on the back of the 2S9s. In twenty minutes it was done. When the first ray of sunlight hit the tops of the tallest trees, all six of the 2S9s were in smoking ruin. And there were no survivors among the crews.

The needle nose of the Tree Toad missile was deflected just enough upward by the beveled edge of the No Slack Too's fender that its warhead, designed to burn through conventional armor, only puddled a furrow through the monopolar skin of the XM-F4, and the secondary blast splattered molten droplets harmlessly in the air.

Ham was already locked on the 2S9 when it fired, and his 120mm sabot found no resistance in the toy tank's defenses, ripping through into the engine and parting the chassis with the force of its explosion.

And now, Ham thought, *Captain Maxman'll be fucking with me for getting a scratch on the Too. Fuck a buncha war.*

"There they are," Tag said.

Porno ran past him, loping for the familiar sound of the No Slack Too's gun. Betcher was banged up and having a harder time of it than he pretended, but Tag thought now they might, just might, make it. And Giesla—Giesla was a rock.

• • •

N. Sain overtook the Soviet main body before it had gone five hundred meters into the forest. In the rising light he could see them, four abreast and four deep, as he stood in the top hatch next to the cupola of the Phalanx. The Roman-square formation was no good for moving fast in forest, but it was difficult for men on foot to penetrate and still too fast for them to catch if the Soviets ran.

He would wait. These were both gifts and offerings, from and for the Dark Divinity. He would know when it was their time to die.

Prentice and his Bradley full of Rangers were within sight of the No Slack Too when Tag, Giesla, and Betcher at last saw the tank themselves, and a minute later they were there.

Betcher was put in the back of Prentice's APC, along with Horst and the other wounded, while Tag, Prentice, Villalobos, and d'Salassi held a quick confab.

D'Salassi said, "Let's beat feet, Captain. You can bet that bunch back in the vil ain't sitting on their hands."

Tag took mental stock of their situation and said, "No. We're still in good shape. We're not going to completely disengage yet.

"Chuck," he said to Prentice, "let's fall back north, toward the road. Wolfman, you put out men with radios about every five hundred meters. If they all make it back without seeing anything, then we go."

Giesla took the driver's seat in the No Slack Too, and Tag turned the raiders north, on a collision course with Gerisimov's Roman square.

• • •

Gerisimov was ready for the closing-gate maneuver, and he dissolved his square by sending out the first and third ranks perpendicular to the line of advance, while the second and fourth ranks peeled off to either side to fill in the gaps. On the right flank, the tanks slowed to await the left flank's coming around in the sweep.

N. Sain saw the Soviet formation unfolding and read their intents perfectly. He heeled hard right and raced for the flank.

The first team of Rangers that Prentice dropped off was less than two klicks from the No Slack Too when they saw the deploying tanks and radioed to Tag. He halted his movement and waited until the second team reported that they were on the flank of a wheeling maneuver of main battle tanks.

Tag called Prentice to him and outlined the situation.

"We'll backside 'em again, Chuck," he said. "String your people out, and we'll roll 'em up for you on the flank."

As the Bradley juked away through the trees, Tag settled back in his commander's chair and told his crew, "Gunner's choice, people. This is for all the marbles."

Steering by dead reckoning, Tag overtook the Soviet left flank within fifteen minutes, just as it was gathering speed to begin its pivot. Coming at the tank anchoring the end of the line from the rear quarter, Tag was in the Soviets' blind spot, and they never saw him coming. He took the T-80 on the run, ordering Ham to fire only when they were within fifty meters. Flame shot from the rear of the Soviet tank as it lurched forward and died.

The next tank in the rank had kept moving blindly ahead, and it too was taken by surprise when the Phalanx opened up with a stream of 37mm ordnance that split its body armor just below the turret ring and filled the crew compartment with hot, howling ricochets and shell fragments. The big tank veered crazily until it crashed into a tree too big to knock down, killing its engine.

N. Sain heard the guns and smiled sweetly to the air. *Now*, he thought, *fullness is all.* He loosed an ATGM from his rack, bound for the T-80 nearest him, and swung the Phalanx in search of his next target.

At either end of the Soviet line, Rangers leapt into action, hitting the big tanks from the rear when they could, and blasting their tracks when they had to, then crawling in close for the coup de grace, grenades down the cannon barrel or a LAW point-blank in the rear grille.

Tag and the No Slack Too ate at the moving flank in chunks, knocking out five of the lumbering T-80s before any of them realized it was not mines or foot troops doing the damage. And by then it was too late.

Krager and his men were having a duck shoot. The tanks on the hinge end of the maneuver had slowed to a crawl, and Krager had six teams in position at once before he gave the order to fire, entirely eliminating the right flank of Gerisimov's formation.

N. Sain slashed along behind the line, taking targets as they came, picking off tanks that broke from the formation and bushwacking those that stayed in place.

Gerisimov was calm, even serene. As word of the attacks on the flanks came in, he felt an increasing sense of relief. The decision was sure now, his fate no longer an anxious mystery. His radio was mad with messages from his tank commanders, their voices filled with fear. He shut off the radio. Gerisimov twisted in his seat and unsnapped the 9mm automatic in the holster on his hip, checked to see that there was a round in the chamber, thumbed back the hammer, put the barrel in his mouth, and blew the top of his head into his helmet.

12

At midmorning, under a bright November sun, on the anniversary of Tag's birth, the No Slack Too and the two Bradleys emerged from the woods and took to the road, heading east. Behind them, smoke rose from the forest from the burning remains of the first battalion of the antitank recon regiment of the First Guards Tank Army.

Giesla adjusted the CVC on her head and said, "What now, Max?"

"I'm taking us in," he said. "Our magazines are nearly empty; we got no more fuel left to scrounge, and Ivan is through in this sector. I'd say we've done our job."

"Well," Giesla said, "show me, then, how do you drive this warthog." She settled her hands on the steering yoke.

•　•　•

Yeshev read the reports coming in from the few survivors of his first battalion with seeming indifference, chain-smoking and drinking black tea. Command had made a bad gamble, and now they would want to cash his chips to pay the debt. He did not think he would do that.

Yeshev waited until noon and still he had not heard from First Guards' headquarters. He called his operations officer over to the corner of the bunker where he sat and said, "Professor, Comrade Minski, would you try to reach command for me, please? I am tired of waiting for the other shoe to drop."

Major Nikolai Viktor, the intelligence officer whom Yeshev had long suspected of being little more than a toady for the security service, ducked into the bunker and stood with his arms akimbo, staring at Yeshev.

"Comrade Colonel," Viktor said, "I am required to tell you that after having observed your counter-revolutionary behavior during the past few weeks, I have been forced to report it to the highest possible quarters. I am, effective immediately, taking command of this regiment and placing you under arrest."

Yeshev looked at Viktor blandly and lit another cigarette. "Very well," he said.

Major Minski stepped from the message desk and stood between the two men.

"Comrade Colonel," he said, holding out a message sheet for Yeshev, "perhaps you should read this first."

Yeshev read the message, blew smoke on it, and picked up the pistol lying on the ammo box beside him. "Here," he said, handing the message to Victor, "read this, Nikolai."

Viktor raised the sheet to his face. Yeshev raised the pistol and shot him twice in the chest.

Minski, who had recoiled at the sound, froze at the door of the bunker. "What was that?"

"That," said Yeshev, putting the pistol down, "was a summary court-martial, comrade, my first official act as acting commander of the First Guards Tanks." Yeshev reached down and took the order from Viktor's dead hand. "Give the order, Professor: white flags and capped tubes. We're through here. I'm taking these men home."

Giesla was a marvel at the controls of the No Slack Too. Tag would not have suspected that the driving skills she had honed in road rallies and Jagd Kommando training would transfer to armor, but she was a natural, the best he had seen since Wheels Latta. They were riding with all the hatches open, Giesla learning to steer by feel alone and doing wondrously at it, Porno with his head out the turret hatch straining the wind through his strong teeth, and Tag looking across the glacis at Giesla. He was a happy man, his joy undercut only by the uncertainty of what lay ahead for them. He knew the war was done, he could feel it in his bones and see it more objectively in the desperate gambit that the First Guards had undertaken. He had faith that Kettle would not waste the lives of the raiders, but he equally feared that the diplomats and politicians might not place such high value on them.

With nothing to slow them, the raiders crossed the nuclear zone in late afternoon and were in sight of the mineworks before dark.

Butch Lawrence, the captain of the Ranger company pulling security for the headquarters, was the first to reach Tag after he was inside the perimeter. Lawrence leapt on the glacis of the No Slack Too and grabbed Tag's hand to shake it.

"It's over, Max," he shouted. "The war's over."

"W-what?" Tag stammered.

"It's over, I'm telling you. We just got the word. Get your people together; I'm supposed to get you all over to see Colonel Barlow, soon as possible."

"Well, I'll be damned," was all Tag could say.

He shook off his shock and quickly called all the raiders together, assembling them outside the mine shaft.

"It's over," he said, and a murmur ran through the ranks. "I said," Tag repeated, "it's over."

This time a cheer went up from the men. They threw their helmets and whooped and slapped one another on the back until Tag called them down.

"Okay, okay," he said. "Colonel Barlow has the full skinny, and I think you all deserve to hear it straight from him. Follow me."

Tag turned and walked into the shaft toward the cavern inside, Giesla on one side of him and Porno padding along on the other.

The raiders spread out behind Tag as they came into the lantern-lit cavern, and Colonel Barlow came from the map table to meet them. He shook hands with Tag and Giesla and Prentice, then looked to the men and said, "Congratulations, all of you. You men have done one hell of a job, and there are plenty who know it, even if most of these operations you've been on never officially happened."

He looked back at Tag and said, "Captain, let your men get comfortable, get some coffee, and I'll tell you all what we know."

While the men dropped their gear and circled

on the coffee urns, Barlow took Tag, Giesla, and
Prentice aside and said, "Something else I thought
you might want to know, even it's not official yet:
the First Guards have given it up on their own, it
seems."

"What do you mean?" Tag said.

"Beginning a little after noon today, we started
getting broadcasts from them in the clear, saying that
they were coming in to surrender. Aerial recon says
that's what it looks like they're doing. They should
start straggling in here sometime tomorrow."

"So, what's unofficial about it, sir?" Prentice
asked.

"SACEUR says that the only one he'll authorize
to accept the surrender is Max here."

They were all silent for a moment, then Tag said,
"Thanks, Colonel. That will be an honor. But come
on, we'd like to hear the rest of it."

The men sprawled on their packs, sipping coffee,
and Tag, Giesla, and Prentice found ammo boxes
for seats.

"The wheels," Barlow said, "have come off Ivan's
war machine, and the political machine has crashed
and burned. I'm sorry that I can't give you all the
details, but I will tell you all I know.

"For several weeks now, we've been getting signals
that the government in Moscow was in trouble, with
lots of popular sentiment running against the war.
Apparently, after the nuclear exchange, things really
got difficult for the party bosses—desertions from the
army, massive draft resistance, protests in the streets,
all sorts of things like that, according to the reports.

"Suddenly, three days ago, there was absolutely nothing coming out of Moscow. Army movements faltered, the peace negotiators canceled their

meetings, and all we knew for certain was that something big was taking place inside the Kremlin. But few if any suspected what would come next.

"Between what we've heard from SACEUR and the reports on the BBC, it appears that there's been a palace revolt. The Svetlovists are back in control of the government and actually asking for Allied aid to help them consolidate their power. They have asked permission to withdraw all their troops and agreed to leave all artillery, tanks, and missiles in place when they do. Less than two hours ago, we got the official order to cease all hostilities."

"And that's it, sir?" Krager asked from the first row of men.

"All but the sweeping up," Barlow said, "but for all of you, yes. Forty-eight hours from now, you'll all be sleeping in beds."

Tag stood and said, "Unless the colonel has something else, you're all dismissed. Get some chow, wash up your scuzzy bodies."

"Max," Barlow said as the briefing broke up, "one thing: what is the story on that gooch-eyed dog or pony or whatever he is?"

"Hey, Colonel," Tag replied, "don't say anything bad about the puppy. That dog loves me."

Porno rose and stretched, snarled at Tag, and slinked off with Fruits and Ham.

"Good thing for you," Barlow said.

The atmosphere was almost festive that evening in the mountain redoubt. The people from the nearby village who had earlier sheltered Tag and his unit showed up with more demijohns of the flowery local wine, and everyone got a little tight. The tall, lame veterinarian from the village who had once treated

Tag's wounded now examined Porno and pronounced him an underfed but marvelous example of a Swabian mastiff whose ears and tail had never been cropped. The pretty twins who tended the kennels at his clinic fell in love with Porno, and he with them, and Fruits was persuaded to go along with the adoption.

"Can't be raising no dog like that in a Bronx tenement, anyway, Tutti Fruity," said Ham, "unless you plannin' on usin' him to accessorize a mugger."

Giesla and Tag caught each other's eye and rose without a word and walked out of the cavern into the chill November night. The moon was up and the sky clear, and they picked their way across the rocky expanse of tailings in front of the mined mountainside, just strolling.

"It is not yet real to me, Max," she said.

"I know," he said. "I don't even know how to think about it, let alone what to think."

"I think I am happy," she said. "I think I am very, very happy."

They walked a ways in silence and stopped in the shadows of the trees on the far side of the tailings and kissed.

"A bed next time," said Giesla. "I think you promised me a bed, Captain."

"If you can control yourself for forty-eight hours, I'll get us the biggest hotel suite in Brussels."

She pushed him playfully in the chest. "Control myself!" she said. "You are a monster of ego, Max Tag."

"Yeah," Tag said, bending his lips into a grin. "Don't ya just love it?"

At 1645 hours the following day, Colonel Feyodr Oblanovich Yeshev entered the perimeter of the mineworks and surrendered his pistol to Captain Maximilian Tag.

"You are Butcher Boy?" Yeshev asked in his thickly accented English.

"Yes," Tag replied.

"Is honor to surrender to you," Yeshev said. "Many things would I like to discuss with you."

Two Rangers stepped beside him and took him by the arms. "Another time, perhaps," he said to Tag.

"Yes," Tag said, "perhaps another time."

World War III will be fought on the ocean floor. The future of military technology has arrived . . .

DEEPCORE

It's the world's first underwater security installation. A marvel of technology, armed to protect America's interests over two-thirds of the Earth, it is our last defense in a new kind of war.

An explosive new novel by James B. Adair, available in November 1991 from Berkley books.

Here's an exclusive preview . . .

Jack Travis was only half listening to the computer tech's report. He was still trying to get used to meeting strangers in the hallways. It seemed unnatural to meet someone he didn't know in a passageway nine hundred feet below the surface of the Pacific. Even watching the big Los Angeles-class submarine dock at the end of the industrial area had not prepared him for the sudden presence of 127 strangers who were like kids in a toy store after months submerged at sea.

For some reason, the Positrack team hadn't been so unsettling. Dr. Brittan, his secretary, and the handful of technicians fit right in. The sub crews were different. Maybe it was just the military aspect of them. Travis had never been too comfortable around military types. Janice Wellford, Brittan's secretary, said she could smell testosterone in the air when the sub docked. That could well be the explanation. The women on DeepCore were the only females these guys had seen in weeks.

Travis forced himself to listen to Will Harper, the computer man. He was explaining the computer interlock system, a concept that Travis understood well, but cared little about.

"And now, with the interlock finally operational," Harper was saying, "we can electronically control access and environment in each module and passage, from dozens of access terminals."

Travis nodded and tried to look interested.

"What the hell is he up to?" Bradley whispered.

"I don't know for sure," Hansen hissed, "but he just took a couple of pictures of the component boards and now he's pulling one of the CPUs apart."

"Think he's just calibrating the components?" Bradley asked.

"I don't know any calibration you can do with a camera. Come on."

The two technicians slipped around the far side of the racks, keeping the equipment between them and Watanabe. When they were directly behind him, both men peered through the stacked boxes. They watched as Watanabe pulled one of the CPUs apart and turned it upside down to expose the circuit board. He put the unit on the table and took out his little camera again, shooting photos of the motherboard from three angles. This done, he slipped the CPU back together and took his power screwdriver to the logic center. When he had the unit disassembled, he pulled the logic board out and laid it on the bench, reaching again for his camera.

When Watanabe's back was turned, Hansen slipped quietly around the rack.

"Whatta'ya up to, Kinji?" Hansen barked.

The little man jumped a foot and spun around.

"You scared me!" he shrieked.

"Yeah?" Hansen asked in mock sympathy. "Sorry about that. Whatta'ya doing with the logic circuits? I thought they were supposed to stay sealed."

"Well, I, uh, I needed to check something on it," Watanabe stammered.

"Really? What?" Hansen began to hammer at the little man, pushing him to see where he would go.

"Well," Watanabe lied, "I was just looking at the differences in these circuits." He reached back on the bench and picked up the board, pointing to one of the tiny gold tracks on the printed circuit board.

"Is that right?" Hansen taunted. "I don't think so, Kinji. I think Dr. Brittan should talk to you about this."

At the mention of Brittan's name, Watanabe paled a bit. "No, I do not think that will be necessary," he said quickly, perspiration beading up on his lip. "We can just—" Watanabe suddenly bolted from the room, still holding the circuit board.

"Come on!" Hansen yelled over his shoulder at Bradley. The two men dashed out of the room after the fleeing man.

When he heard the voice behind him, he had almost crawled out of his skin. His skin had felt like it really was moving, a hot, prickly feeling that only lasted a second. Now, with the big American technician standing practically on top of him, Watanabe felt his heart pounding. The hot, prickly feeling gave way to a cold terror. The American's sarcastic tone was making the feeling worse. Dread was replacing simple fear. He could hear himself babbling out some simpleminded excuse, his mind racing to concoct some plausible story for dismantling one of the classified components.

The possibility of Brittan's involvement turned the dread into panic. Brittan was the boss. If he got involved, it was good-bye Watanabe. Without thinking, he picked up the logic board, mouthed something about circuits, and bolted for the door. As he cleared the lab storage area, he could hear Hansen and another man, probably Bradley, behind him.

Watanabe fished in his lab-coat pocket for his only weapon, the small hyper-velocity pistol. The gun looked less like a gun than anything he had ever seen. Although it was just a single shot, it was deadly at close range. It had been developed for the Japanese Secret Service a year or so before. The Japanese had never lost one and had never shared the secrets of its development with others.

Reaching the connecting corridor, Watanabe pulled the door shut and ran down to the porthole near the far end of the corridor. He pulled the tiny hyper-velocity pistol from his pocket and pointed it at the center of the porthole. Covering his face with his other hand, Watanabe pulled the trigger. The noise from the tiny pistol was more of a loud pop, but the sliver of depleted uranium left the muzzle at over three thousand feet per second. Watanabe did not even glance at the porthole. At the far end of the corridor, Hansen and Bradley burst through the pressure door. Watanabe slipped through the door at his end and slammed it shut, spinning the lock wheel. The two technicians hit the door handle just as the locking bolts went home. Watanabe could hear the men shouting at him, the words muffled, but the

intention plain. Hansen hit the door with his fist
as Bradley put all his weight on the locking wheel
to unlock the door. On his side, Watanabe fought
hard to keep the wheel from turning. Hansen's size
and strength were beginning to overcome Watanabe's
when the porthole blew in behind the two men. Under
the crushing pressure, the broken porthole became a
cylinder of water, a jet that blew the paint off the
wall and scattered the flooring grids like confetti in
a tornado.

The flood control system activated instantly, a compressed air piston slamming shut the open pressure
door at the far end of the corridor. Hansen and
Bradley were trapped by the eighteen-inch column
of water that continued to blast in from the open
porthole, glancing off the far wall of the corridor
in a fan of high-pressure seawater that knocked both
men off their feet. Bradley managed to get to the
other side of the stream. He slogged through the
rising water toward the far door, but the automatic
system was too fast. The door slammed shut and
automatically locked just as he reached it. Bradley
hammered on the door control with his fist, but the
system was designed to resist pressure of all sorts.
In ten seconds the entire section was sealed off and
flooded.

Through the tiny door porthole, Watanabe saw a
brief flash of Hansen's terrified face, then it was
gone and he could see no sign of either man. He
knew they were dead. No one could survive the icy
water.

Alarms were booming throughout the complex
now. The terminal in each building would display
the break. In a minute the place would be alive
with rescuers and engineers. Watanabe ran around

the corner, stepped up on a conduit, and slipped the circuit board up under a ceiling tile. It would be safe there until the panic subsided. He would retrieve it then.

By the time Jack Travis arrived, the rescue team was already at work. They were in no hurry, because there was obviously no one alive to rescue. The team was now just trying to get the water out of the flooded corridor so they could seal the hole outside. Nancy Collins, the senior engineer, was talking on the com-line to two divers in a submersible that was just launching from the sub pool.

"Okay, let us know when you find the break, over."

"Roger, out."

"What happened, Nancy?" Travis rasped as tried to catch his breath after the panicky sprint from the command center.

"Some sort of break," Collins answered distractedly, standing back to let the two men pulling the emergency compressor pass. "Puncture, maybe."

"Anyone hurt?"

"Hansen, Bradley, and Watanabe were in the lab," Collins replied, ticking the names off her fingers, "we don't get any answer from the lab at all."

"Jesus."

The rescue squad had the compressor hooked up now, its woven steel hose clamped into a fitting on the pressure door. The compressor came on with a deafening clatter, pumping high-pressure air back into the flooded compartment. The small porthole in the door showed a cloud of bubbles rising from the air fitting.

"When we get the cap in place, we'll be able to pump out the water instead of just blowing in air. If the other door is closed, we should see some daylight in there in about half an hour," Collins explained. "If it didn't, it'll take a while to pump out the whole lab."

The thought of the entire lab, including the Positrack project, filled with seawater made Travis sick to his stomach. Aside from the damage to the facility, the hassle they would have with the Navy over the destroyed Positrack gear would be memorable. A scene from an old slasher film flickered through his mind, a pale specter with pins sticking out of his face saying, "Your suffering will be legendary, even in hell."

I'll probably envy that guy, Travis thought gloomily.

"Got something!" one of the rescue crew called. He stepped back from the door's porthole as Collins stepped up.

"Aw, shit," Collins moaned. "Looks like a dead one."

"Who?" Travis snapped, crowding next to Collins. "Who is it?"

"Can't tell," Collins answered, her face still pressed to the glass, "can only see an arm. Wait. Shit!" Collins turned away from the glass, her face torqued with painful recognition.

"It's Hansen," she said, "I recognize his watch." Collins held up her big Rolex Submariner. "It's just like mine."

Travis looked through the glass and caught a glimpse of the bare arm. It looked inhuman in the greenish glow cast by the emergency lights in the flooded corridor. Travis could not see the watch and didn't care to. He stepped back from the glass as the taste of bile rose in his throat and a chill ran up his spine.

"Call me when you get in there," Travis said over his shoulder, walking quickly away down the corridor. "I'll be in the command center."

"Roger that," Collins said to her boss's retreating back.